RL:3.Y

Coloring in
Doodle 1/22
Water damage
6/21/22 RU

D1443768

Sir Arthur Conan Doyle's
The Adventure of the Red-Headed League

Adapted by: Vincent Goodwin

Illustrated by: Ben Dunn

magic wagon

visit us at
www.abdopublishing.com

Published by Magic Wagon, a division of the ABDO Group, 8000 West 78th Street, Edina, Minnesota, 55439.

Printed in the United States of America, North Mankato, Minnesota.
102009
012010

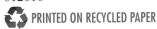

PRINTED ON RECYCLED PAPER

Original novel by Sir Arthur Conan Doyle
Adapted by Vincent Goodwin
Illustrated by Ben Dunn
Colored by Robby Bevard
Edited by Stephanie Hedlund and Rochelle Baltzer
Interior layout and design by Antarctic Press
Cover art by Ben Dunn
Cover design by Abbey Fitzgerald

Library of Congress Cataloging-in-Publication Data

Goodwin, Vincent.
Sir Arthur Conan Doyle's The adventure of the Red-Headed League / adapted by Vincent Goodwin ; illustrated by Ben Dunn.
p. cm. -- (The graphic novel adventures of Sherlock Holmes)
Summary: Retells in graphic novel format a story featuring the great English detective Sherlock Holmes.
Includes bibliographical references.
ISBN 978-1-60270-726-9
1. Graphic novels. [1. Graphic novels. 2. Doyle, Arthur Conan, Sir, 1859-1930. Red-Headed League—Adaptations. 3. Mystery and detective stories.] I. Dunn, Ben, ill. II. Doyle, Arthur Conan, Sir, 1859-1930. Adventure of the red-headed league. III. Title. IV. Title: Adventure of the Red-Headed League.

PZ7.7.G66Si 2010
741.5'973--dc22

2009032460

Table of Contents

Cast

Sherlock Holmes

Dr. John Watson

Jabez Wilson

Vincent Spaulding

Duncan Ross

Mister Jones

Mister Merryweather

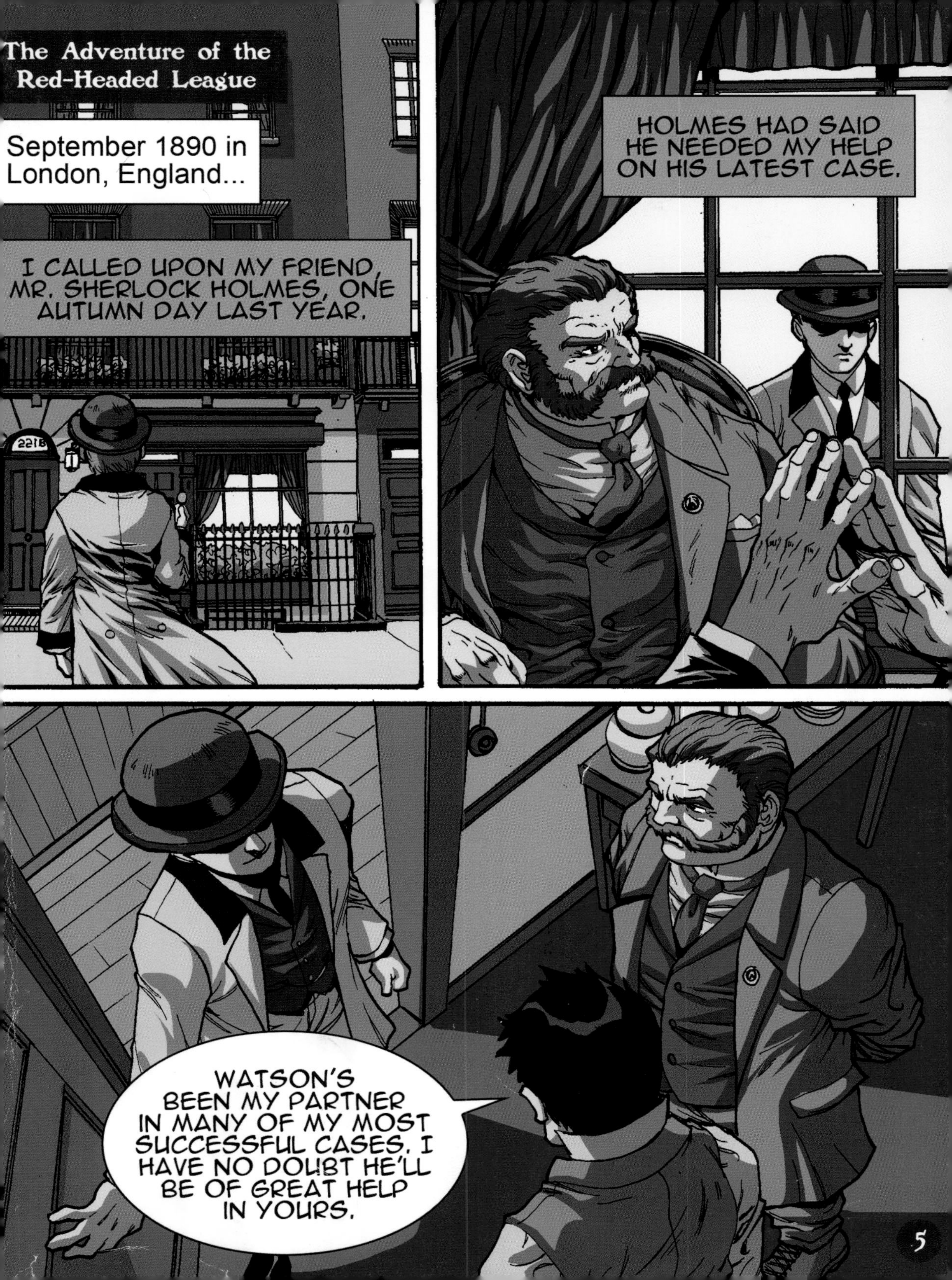
The Adventure of the Red-Headed League
September 1890 in London, England...
I CALLED UPON MY FRIEND, MR. SHERLOCK HOLMES, ONE AUTUMN DAY LAST YEAR.
221B
HOLMES HAD SAID HE NEEDED MY HELP ON HIS LATEST CASE.
WATSON'S BEEN MY PARTNER IN MANY OF MY MOST SUCCESSFUL CASES. I HAVE NO DOUBT HE'LL BE OF GREAT HELP IN YOURS.

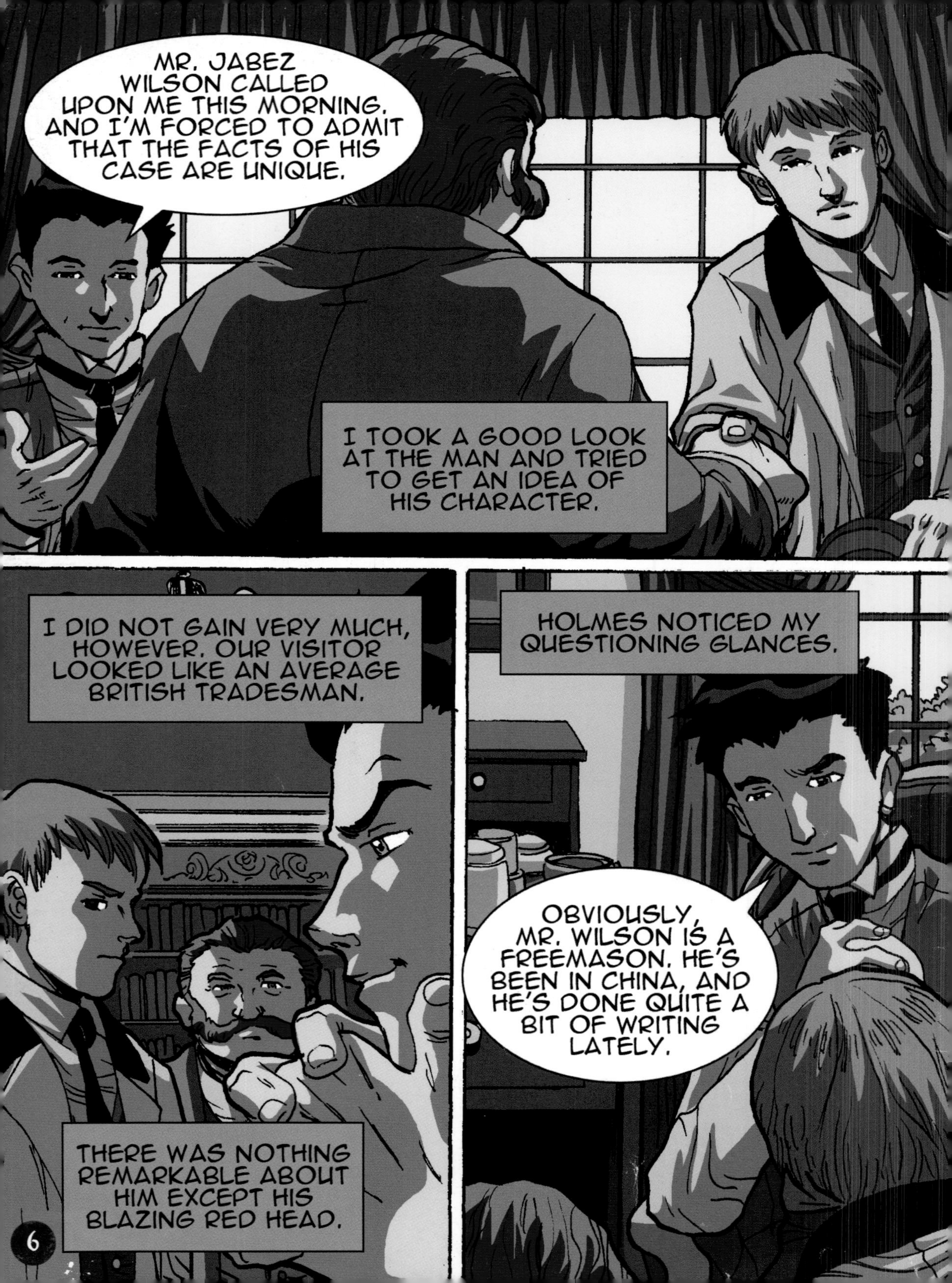
MR. JABEZ WILSON CALLED UPON ME THIS MORNING. AND I'M FORCED TO ADMIT THAT THE FACTS OF HIS CASE ARE UNIQUE.
I TOOK A GOOD LOOK AT THE MAN AND TRIED TO GET AN IDEA OF HIS CHARACTER.
I DID NOT GAIN VERY MUCH, HOWEVER. OUR VISITOR LOOKED LIKE AN AVERAGE BRITISH TRADESMAN.
THERE WAS NOTHING REMARKABLE ABOUT HIM EXCEPT HIS BLAZING RED HEAD.
HOLMES NOTICED MY QUESTIONING GLANCES.
OBVIOUSLY, MR. WILSON IS A FREEMASON. HE'S BEEN IN CHINA, AND HE'S DONE QUITE A BIT OF WRITING LATELY.

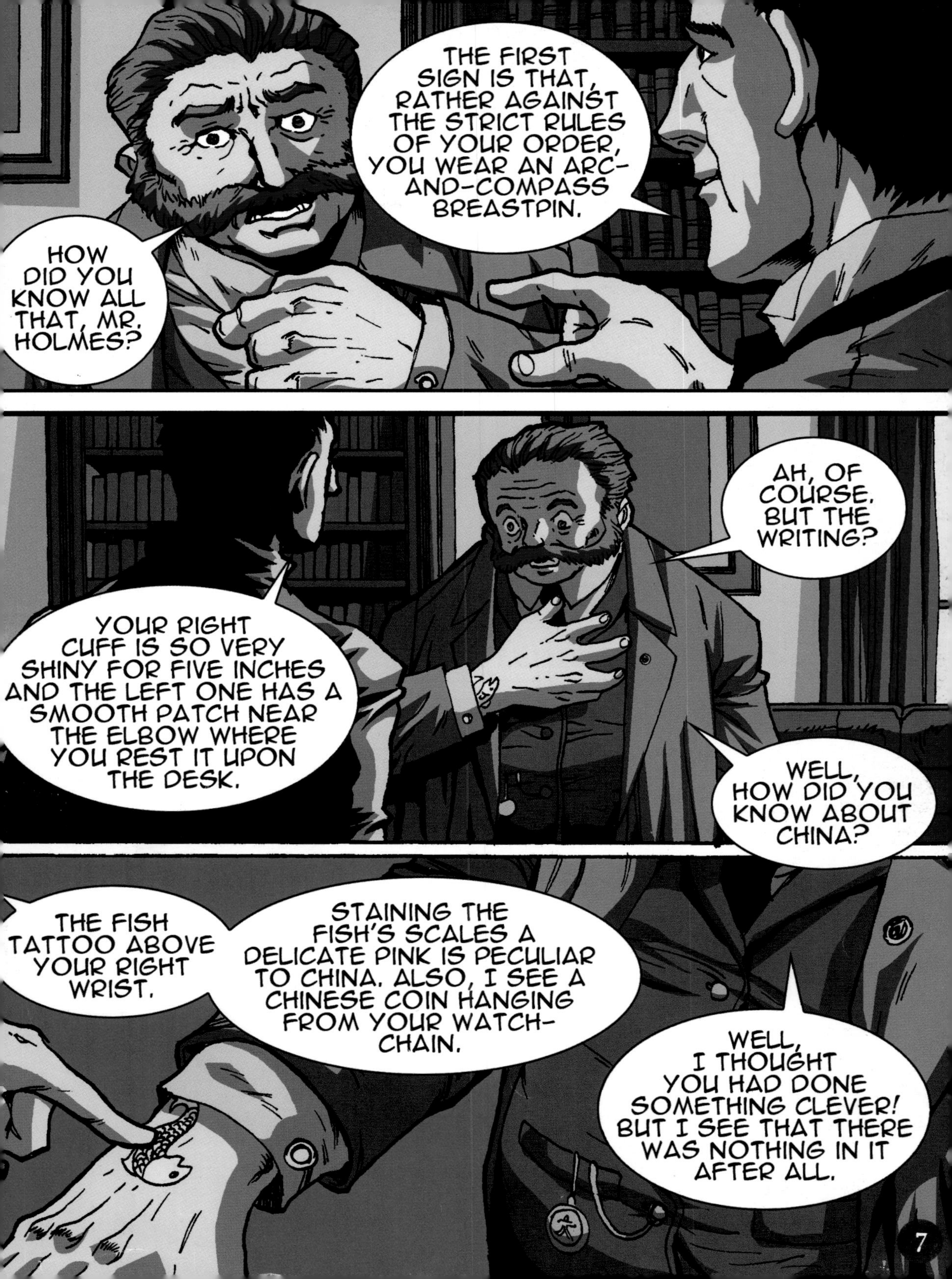
THE FIRST SIGN IS THAT, RATHER AGAINST THE STRICT RULES OF YOUR ORDER, YOU WEAR AN ARC-AND-COMPASS BREASTPIN.
HOW DID YOU KNOW ALL THAT, MR. HOLMES?
AH, OF COURSE. BUT THE WRITING?
YOUR RIGHT CUFF IS SO VERY SHINY FOR FIVE INCHES AND THE LEFT ONE HAS A SMOOTH PATCH NEAR THE ELBOW WHERE YOU REST IT UPON THE DESK.
WELL, HOW DID YOU KNOW ABOUT CHINA?
THE FISH TATTOO ABOVE YOUR RIGHT WRIST.
STAINING THE FISH'S SCALES A DELICATE PINK IS PECULIAR TO CHINA. ALSO, I SEE A CHINESE COIN HANGING FROM YOUR WATCH-CHAIN.
WELL, I THOUGHT YOU HAD DONE SOMETHING CLEVER! BUT I SEE THAT THERE WAS NOTHING IN IT AFTER ALL.

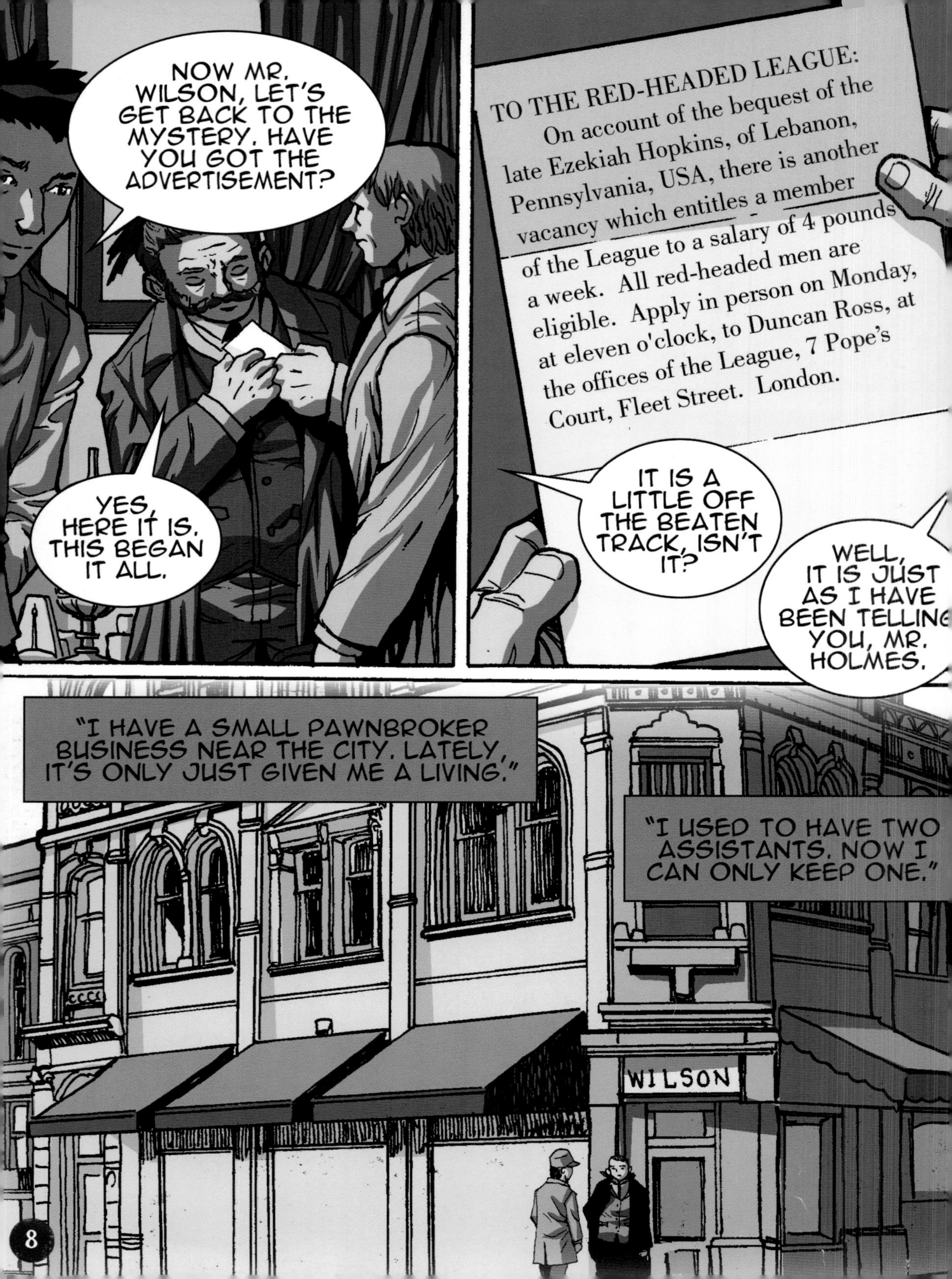
NOW MR. WILSON, LET'S GET BACK TO THE MYSTERY. HAVE YOU GOT THE ADVERTISEMENT?
YES, HERE IT IS. THIS BEGAN IT ALL.
TO THE RED-HEADED LEAGUE:
On account of the bequest of the late Ezekiah Hopkins, of Lebanon, Pennsylvania, USA, there is another vacancy which entitles a member of the League to a salary of 4 pounds a week. All red-headed men are eligible. Apply in person on Monday, at eleven o'clock, to Duncan Ross, at the offices of the League, 7 Pope's Court, Fleet Street. London.
IT IS A LITTLE OFF THE BEATEN TRACK, ISN'T IT?
WELL, IT IS JUST AS I HAVE BEEN TELLING YOU, MR. HOLMES.
"I HAVE A SMALL PAWNBROKER BUSINESS NEAR THE CITY. LATELY, IT'S ONLY JUST GIVEN ME A LIVING."
"I USED TO HAVE TWO ASSISTANTS. NOW I CAN ONLY KEEP ONE."
WILSON

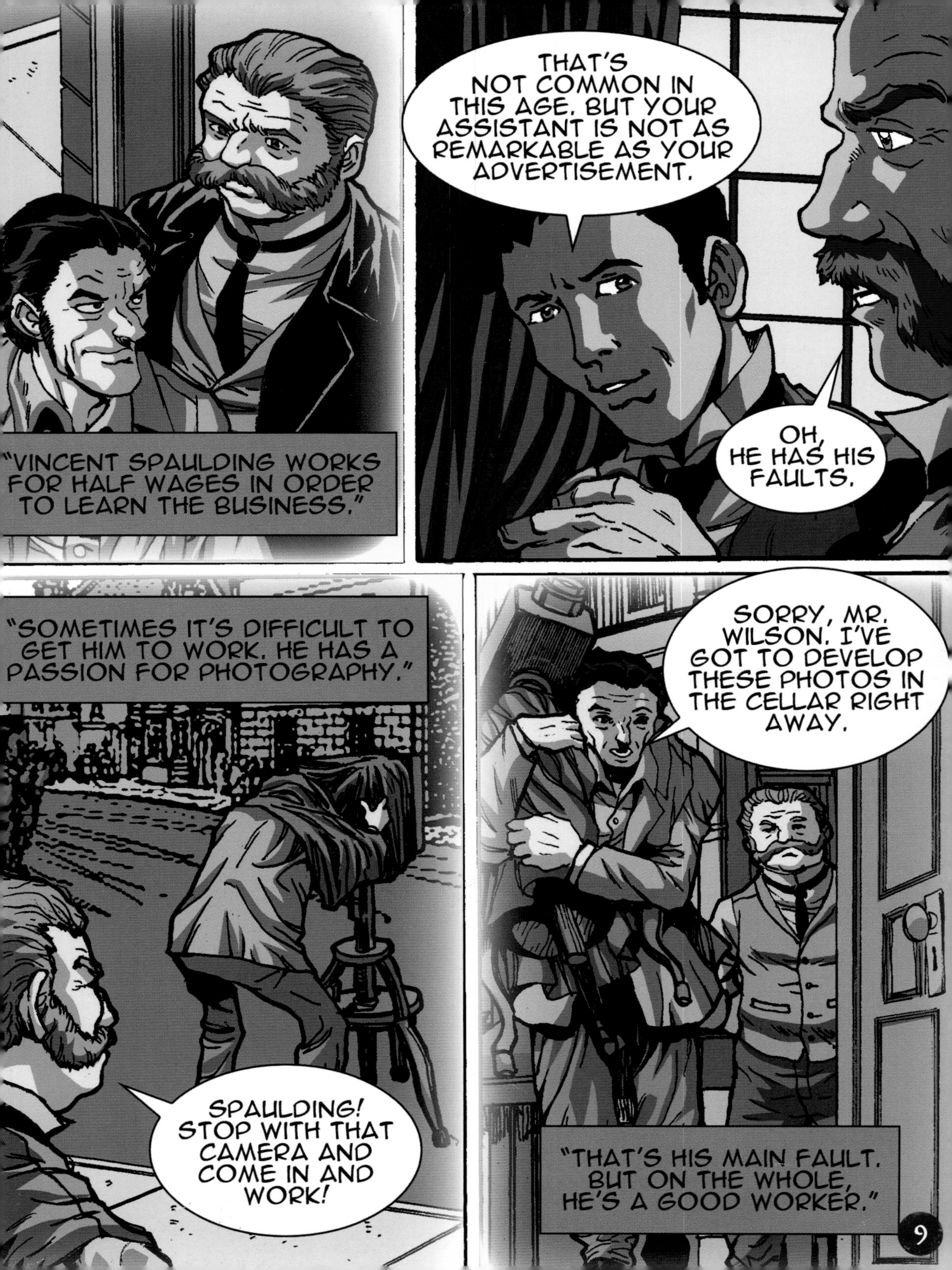

"VINCENT SPAULDING WORKS FOR HALF WAGES IN ORDER TO LEARN THE BUSINESS."
THAT'S NOT COMMON IN THIS AGE. BUT YOUR ASSISTANT IS NOT AS REMARKABLE AS YOUR ADVERTISEMENT.
OH, HE HAS HIS FAULTS.
"SOMETIMES IT'S DIFFICULT TO GET HIM TO WORK. HE HAS A PASSION FOR PHOTOGRAPHY."
SPAULDING! STOP WITH THAT CAMERA AND COME IN AND WORK!
SORRY, MR. WILSON. I'VE GOT TO DEVELOP THESE PHOTOS IN THE CELLAR RIGHT AWAY.
"THAT'S HIS MAIN FAULT. BUT ON THE WHOLE, HE'S A GOOD WORKER."

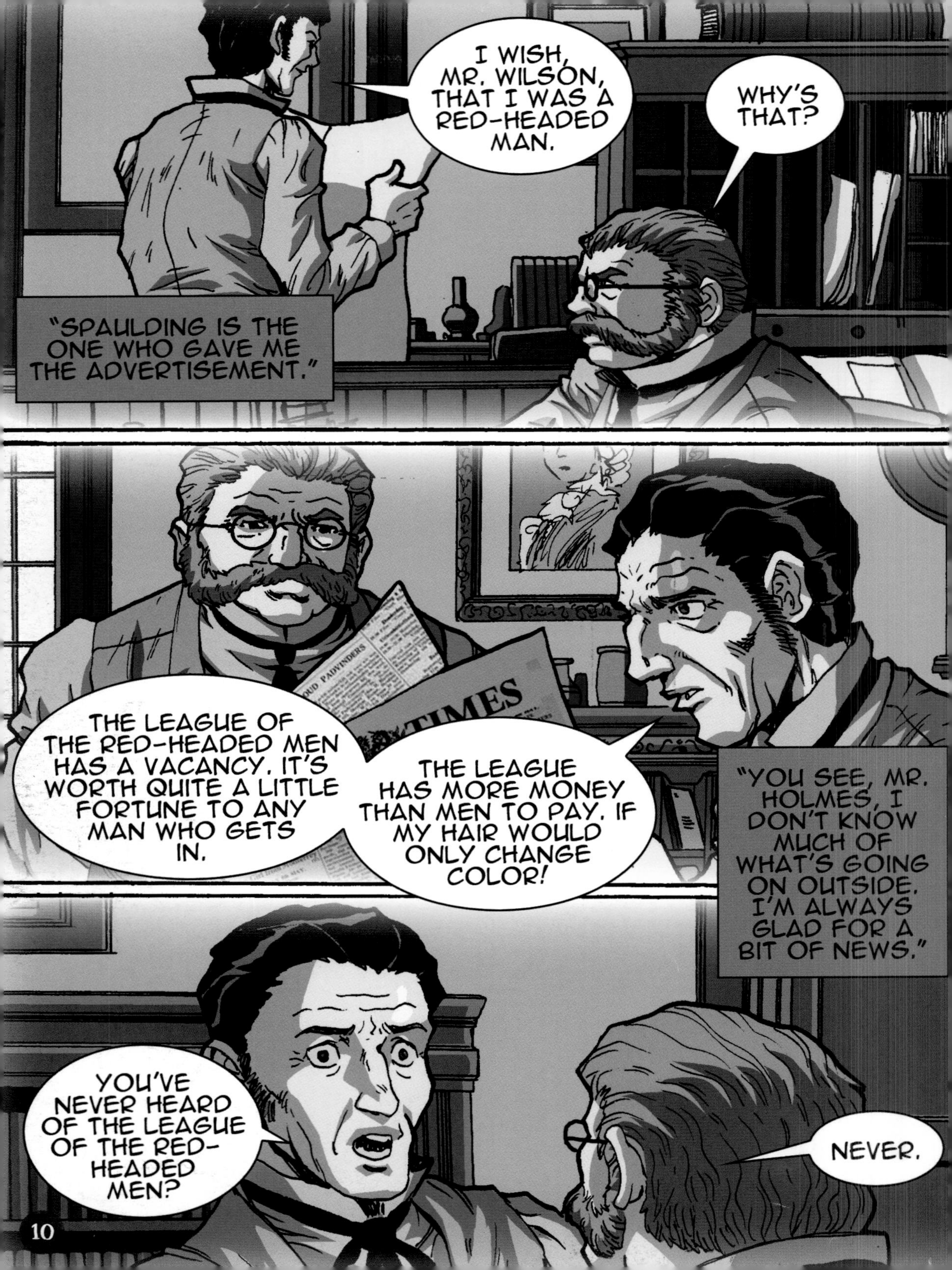
I WISH, MR. WILSON, THAT I WAS A RED-HEADED MAN.
WHY'S THAT?
"SPAULDING IS THE ONE WHO GAVE ME THE ADVERTISEMENT."
TIMES
THE LEAGUE OF THE RED-HEADED MEN HAS A VACANCY. IT'S WORTH QUITE A LITTLE FORTUNE TO ANY MAN WHO GETS IN.
THE LEAGUE HAS MORE MONEY THAN MEN TO PAY. IF MY HAIR WOULD ONLY CHANGE COLOR!
"YOU SEE, MR. HOLMES, I DON'T KNOW MUCH OF WHAT'S GOING ON OUTSIDE. I'M ALWAYS GLAD FOR A BIT OF NEWS."
YOU'VE NEVER HEARD OF THE LEAGUE OF THE RED-HEADED MEN?
NEVER.

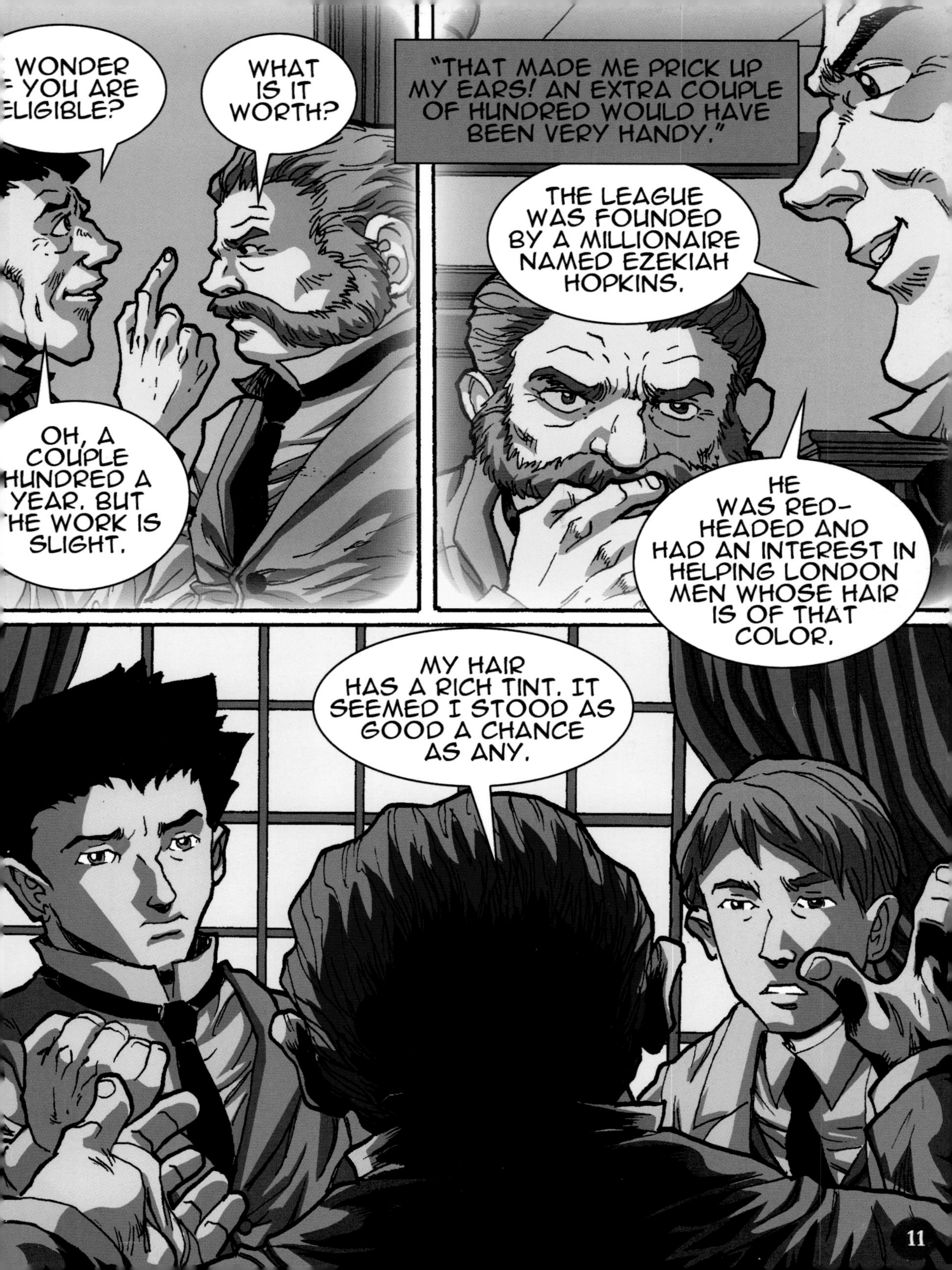

WONDER F YOU ARE ELIGIBLE?
WHAT IS IT WORTH?
OH, A COUPLE HUNDRED A YEAR. BUT HE WORK IS SLIGHT.
"THAT MADE ME PRICK UP MY EARS! AN EXTRA COUPLE OF HUNDRED WOULD HAVE BEEN VERY HANDY."
THE LEAGUE WAS FOUNDED BY A MILLIONAIRE NAMED EZEKIAH HOPKINS.
HE WAS RED-HEADED AND HAD AN INTEREST IN HELPING LONDON MEN WHOSE HAIR IS OF THAT COLOR.
MY HAIR HAS A RICH TINT. IT SEEMED I STOOD AS GOOD A CHANCE AS ANY.

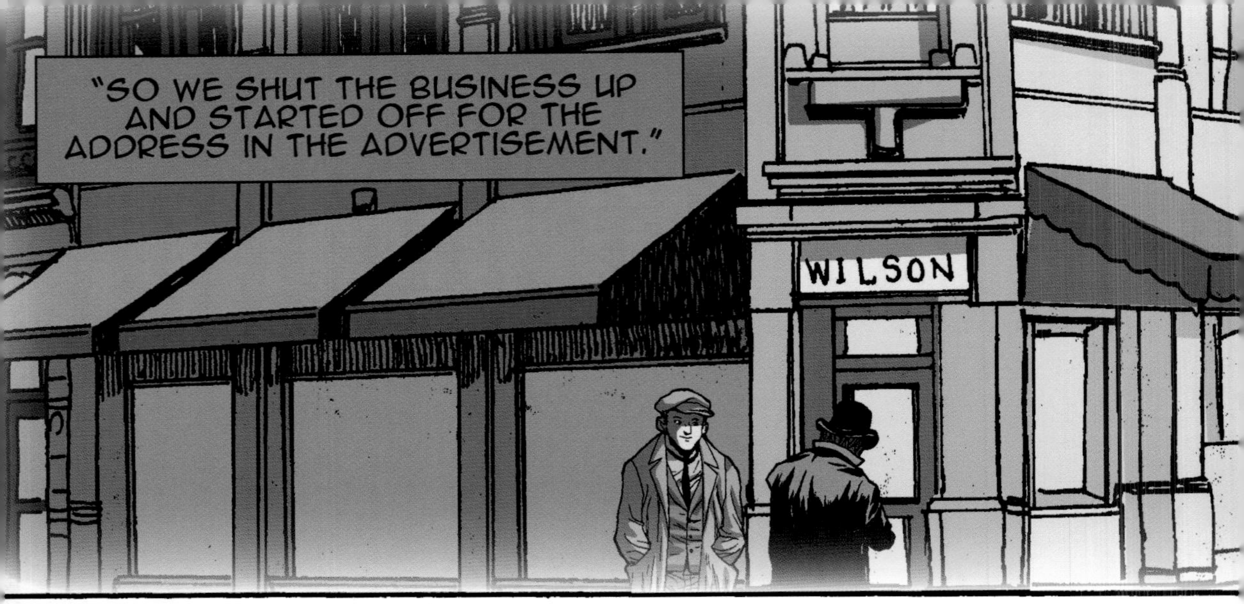
"SO WE SHUT THE BUSINESS UP AND STARTED OFF FOR THE ADDRESS IN THE ADVERTISEMENT."
WILSON

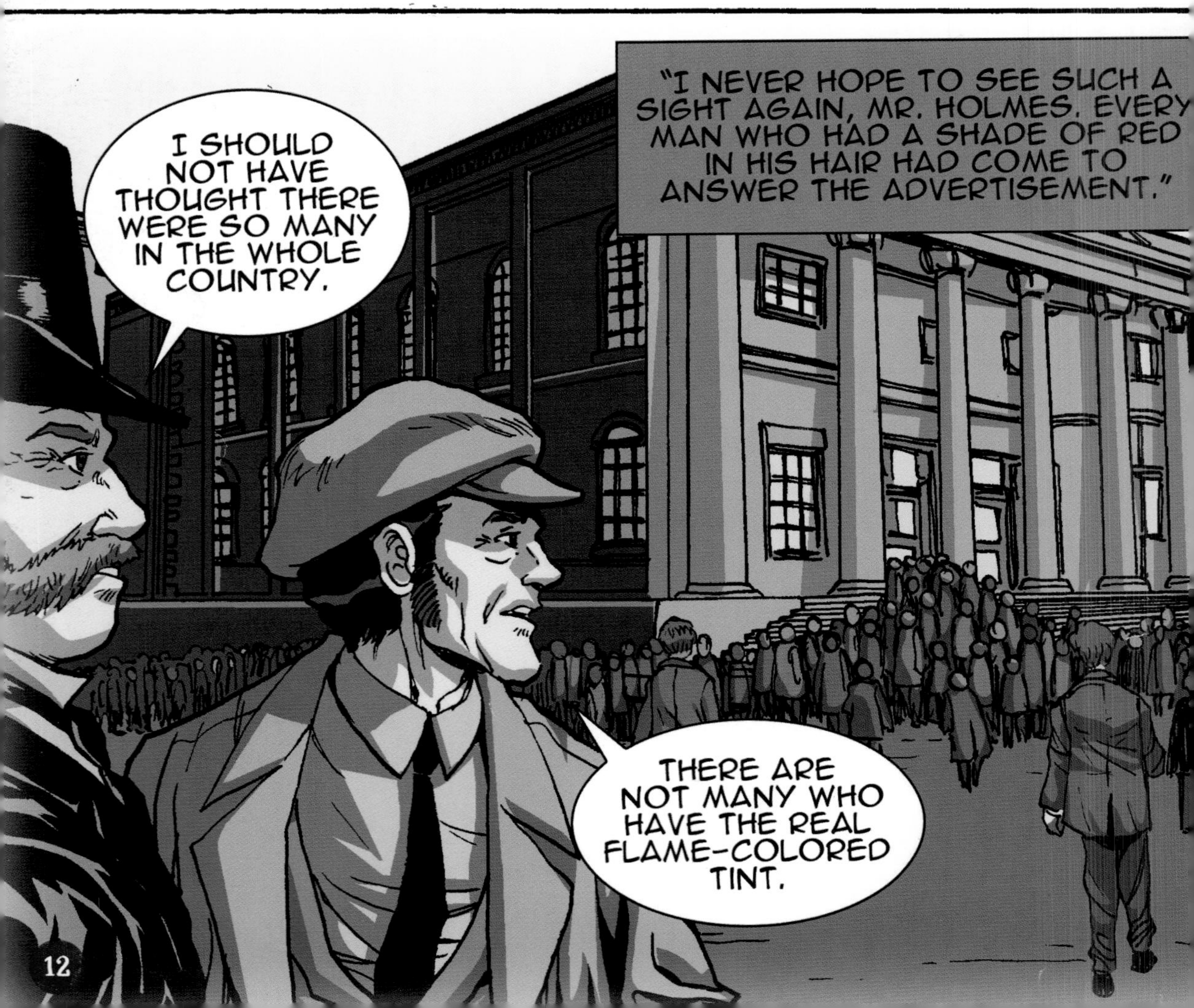
"I NEVER HOPE TO SEE SUCH A SIGHT AGAIN, MR. HOLMES. EVERY MAN WHO HAD A SHADE OF RED IN HIS HAIR HAD COME TO ANSWER THE ADVERTISEMENT."
I SHOULD NOT HAVE THOUGHT THERE WERE SO MANY IN THE WHOLE COUNTRY.
THERE ARE NOT MANY WHO HAVE THE REAL FLAME-COLORED TINT.

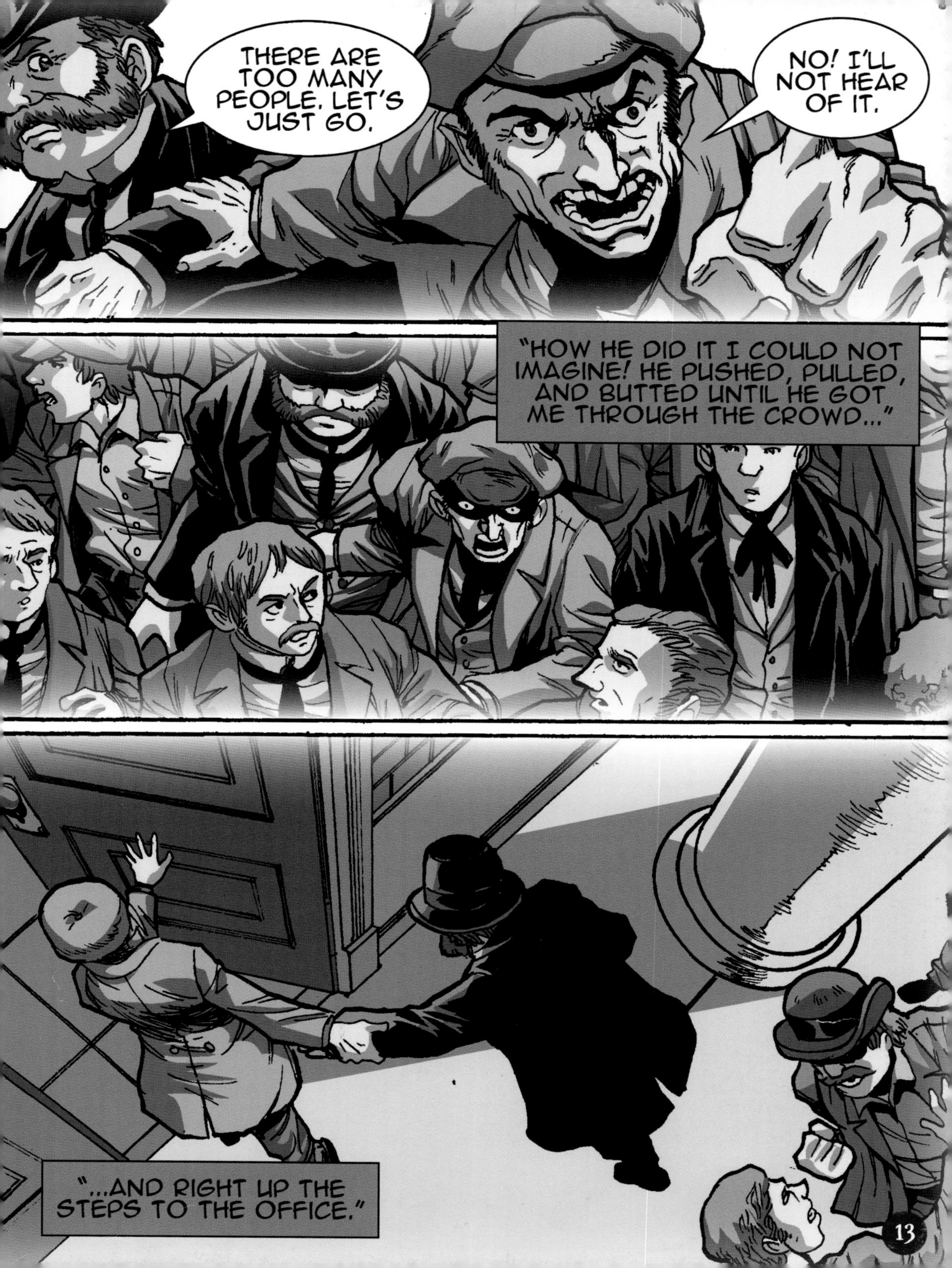
THERE ARE TOO MANY PEOPLE. LET'S JUST GO.
NO! I'LL NOT HEAR OF IT.
"HOW HE DID IT I COULD NOT IMAGINE! HE PUSHED, PULLED, AND BUTTED UNTIL HE GOT ME THROUGH THE CROWD..."
"...AND RIGHT UP THE STEPS TO THE OFFICE."

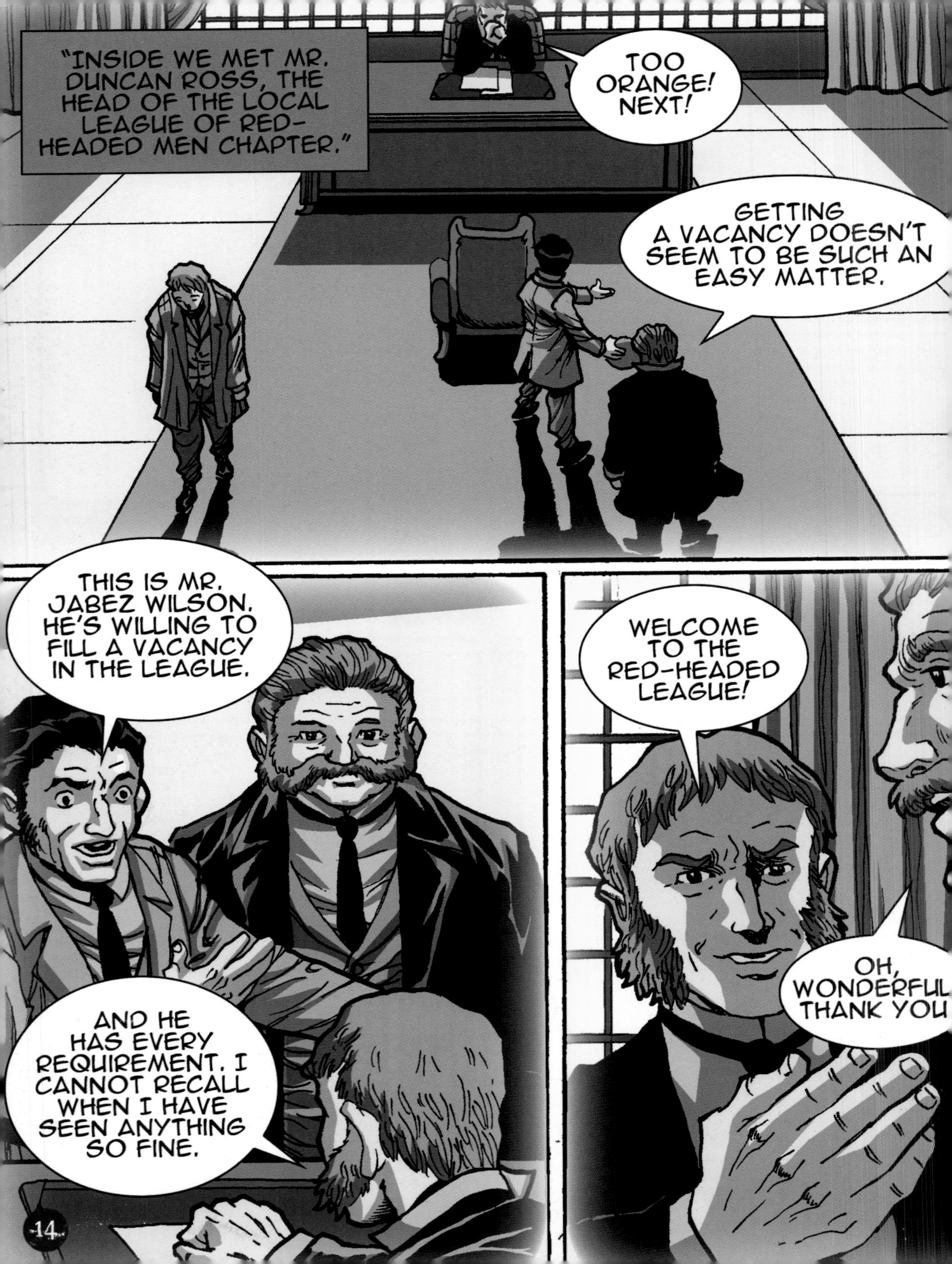
"INSIDE WE MET MR. DUNCAN ROSS, THE HEAD OF THE LOCAL LEAGUE OF RED-HEADED MEN CHAPTER."
TOO ORANGE! NEXT!
GETTING A VACANCY DOESN'T SEEM TO BE SUCH AN EASY MATTER.
THIS IS MR. JABEZ WILSON. HE'S WILLING TO FILL A VACANCY IN THE LEAGUE.
AND HE HAS EVERY REQUIREMENT. I CANNOT RECALL WHEN I HAVE SEEN ANYTHING SO FINE.
WELCOME TO THE RED-HEADED LEAGUE!
OH, WONDERFUL THANK YOU

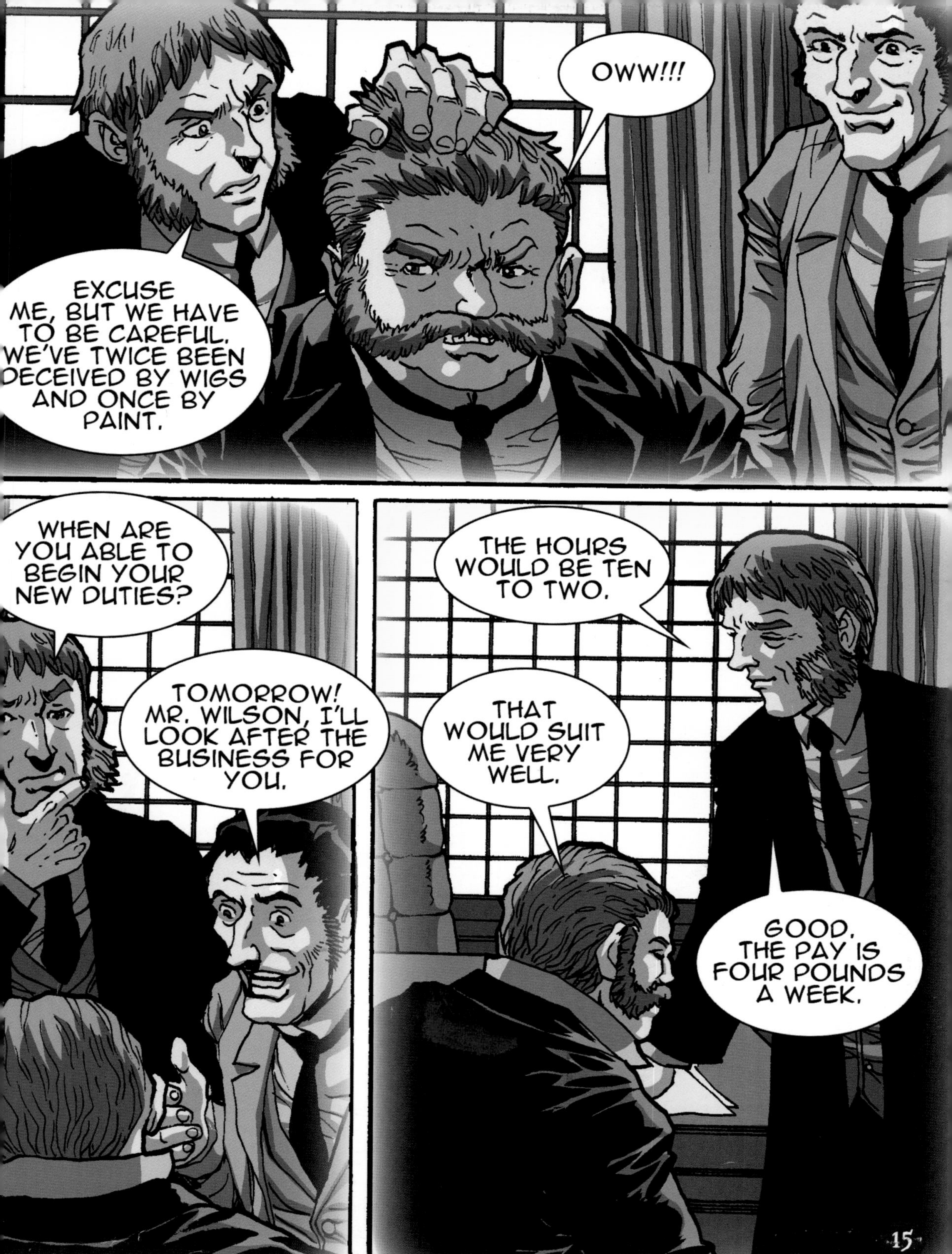
OWW!!!
EXCUSE ME, BUT WE HAVE TO BE CAREFUL. WE'VE TWICE BEEN DECEIVED BY WIGS AND ONCE BY PAINT.
WHEN ARE YOU ABLE TO BEGIN YOUR NEW DUTIES?
TOMORROW! MR. WILSON, I'LL LOOK AFTER THE BUSINESS FOR YOU.
THE HOURS WOULD BE TEN TO TWO.
THAT WOULD SUIT ME VERY WELL.
GOOD. THE PAY IS FOUR POUNDS A WEEK.

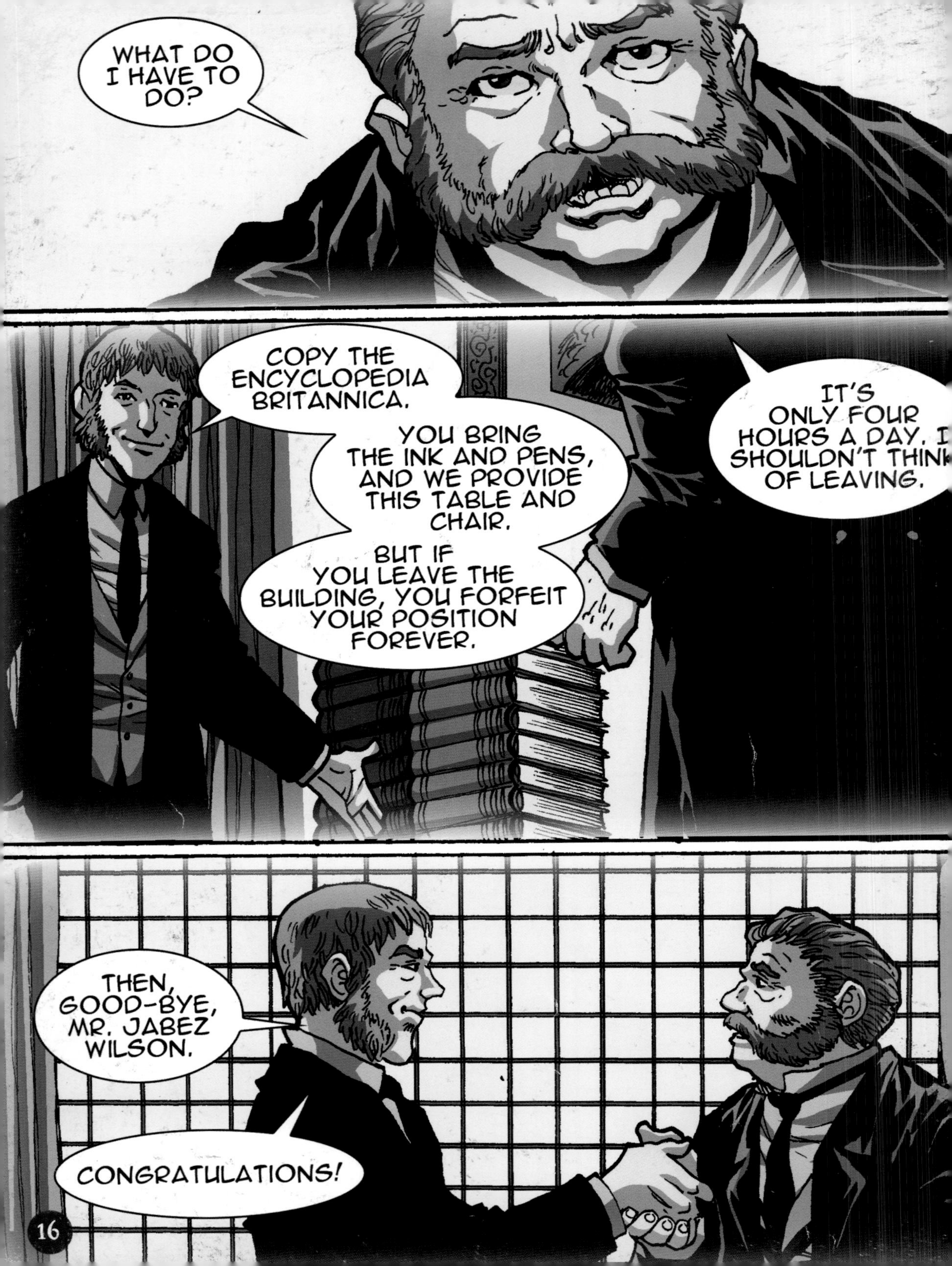
WHAT DO I HAVE TO DO?
COPY THE ENCYCLOPEDIA BRITANNICA.
YOU BRING THE INK AND PENS, AND WE PROVIDE THIS TABLE AND CHAIR.
BUT IF YOU LEAVE THE BUILDING, YOU FORFEIT YOUR POSITION FOREVER.
IT'S ONLY FOUR HOURS A DAY. I SHOULDN'T THINK OF LEAVING.
THEN, GOOD-BYE, MR. JABEZ WILSON.
CONGRATULATIONS!

IT'S UNBELIEVABLE THAT THERE'S A LEAGUE FOR COPYING THE ENCYCLOPEDIA BRITANNICA!

MILLIONAIRES ARE STRANGE PEOPLE.

THE VACANCY FOR THE RED-HEADED LEAGUE HAS BEEN FILLED!

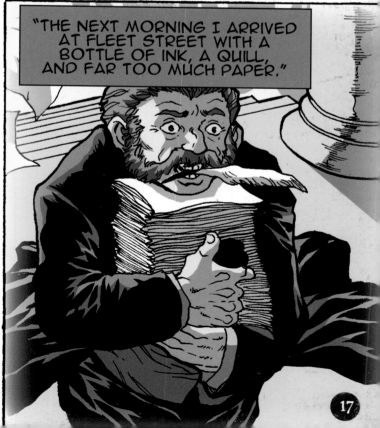

"THE NEXT MORNING I ARRIVED AT FLEET STREET WITH A BOTTLE OF INK, A QUILL, AND FAR TOO MUCH PAPER."

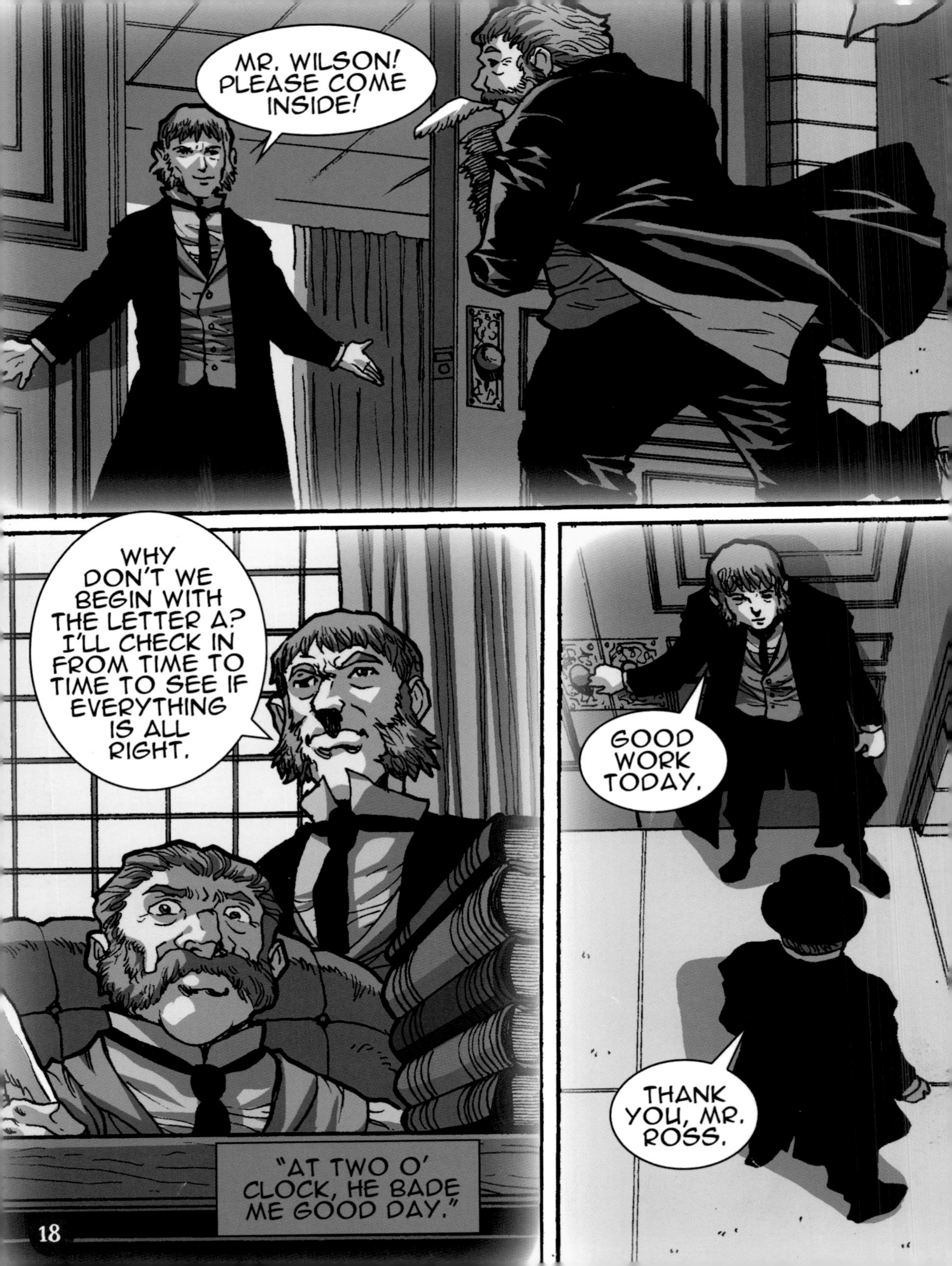
MR. WILSON! PLEASE COME INSIDE!
WHY DON'T WE BEGIN WITH THE LETTER A? I'LL CHECK IN FROM TIME TO TIME TO SEE IF EVERYTHING IS ALL RIGHT.
"AT TWO O' CLOCK, HE BADE ME GOOD DAY."
GOOD WORK TODAY.
THANK YOU, MR. ROSS.

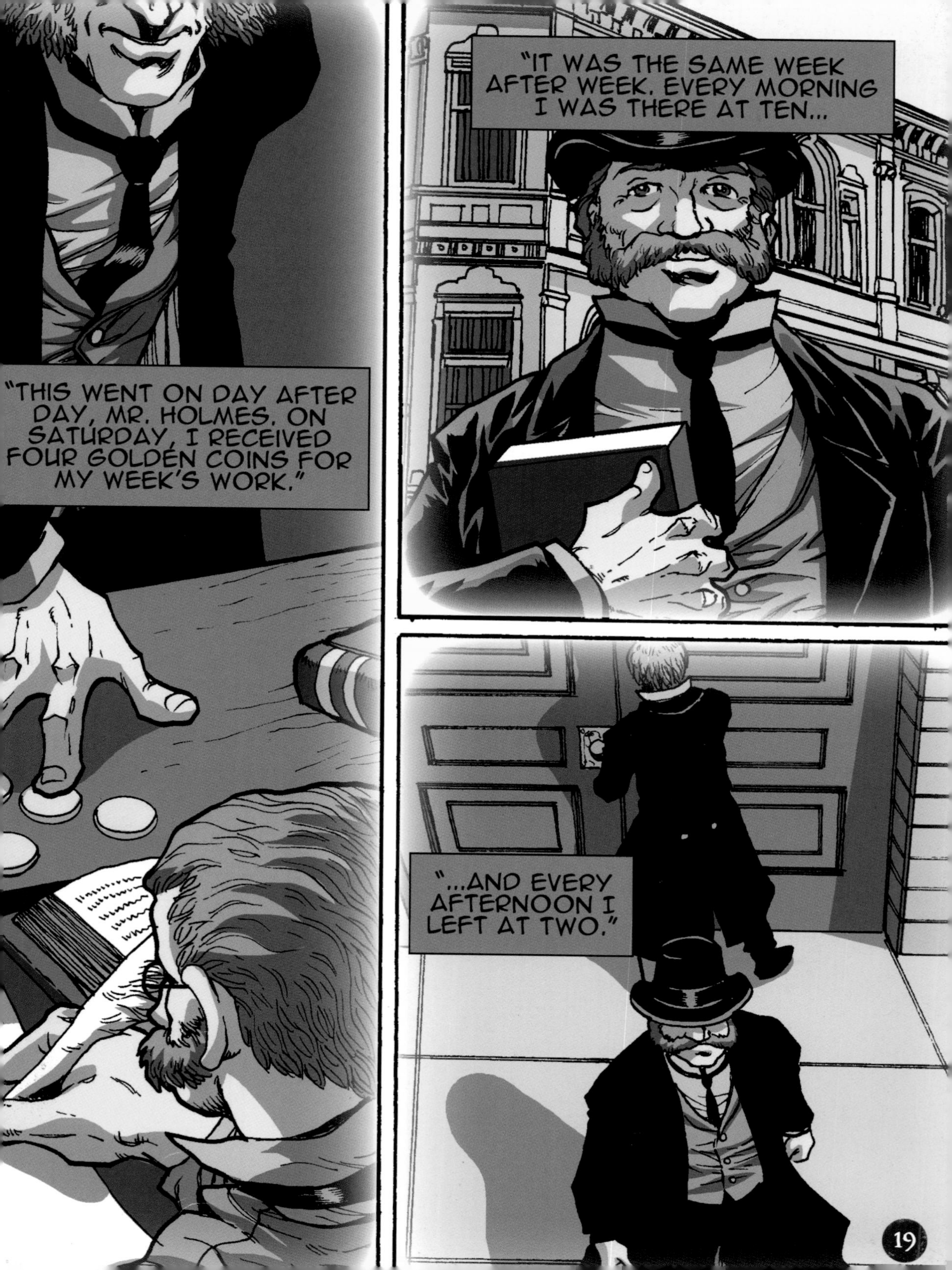
"THIS WENT ON DAY AFTER DAY, MR. HOLMES. ON SATURDAY, I RECEIVED FOUR GOLDEN COINS FOR MY WEEK'S WORK."
"IT WAS THE SAME WEEK AFTER WEEK. EVERY MORNING I WAS THERE AT TEN...
"...AND EVERY AFTERNOON I LEFT AT TWO."

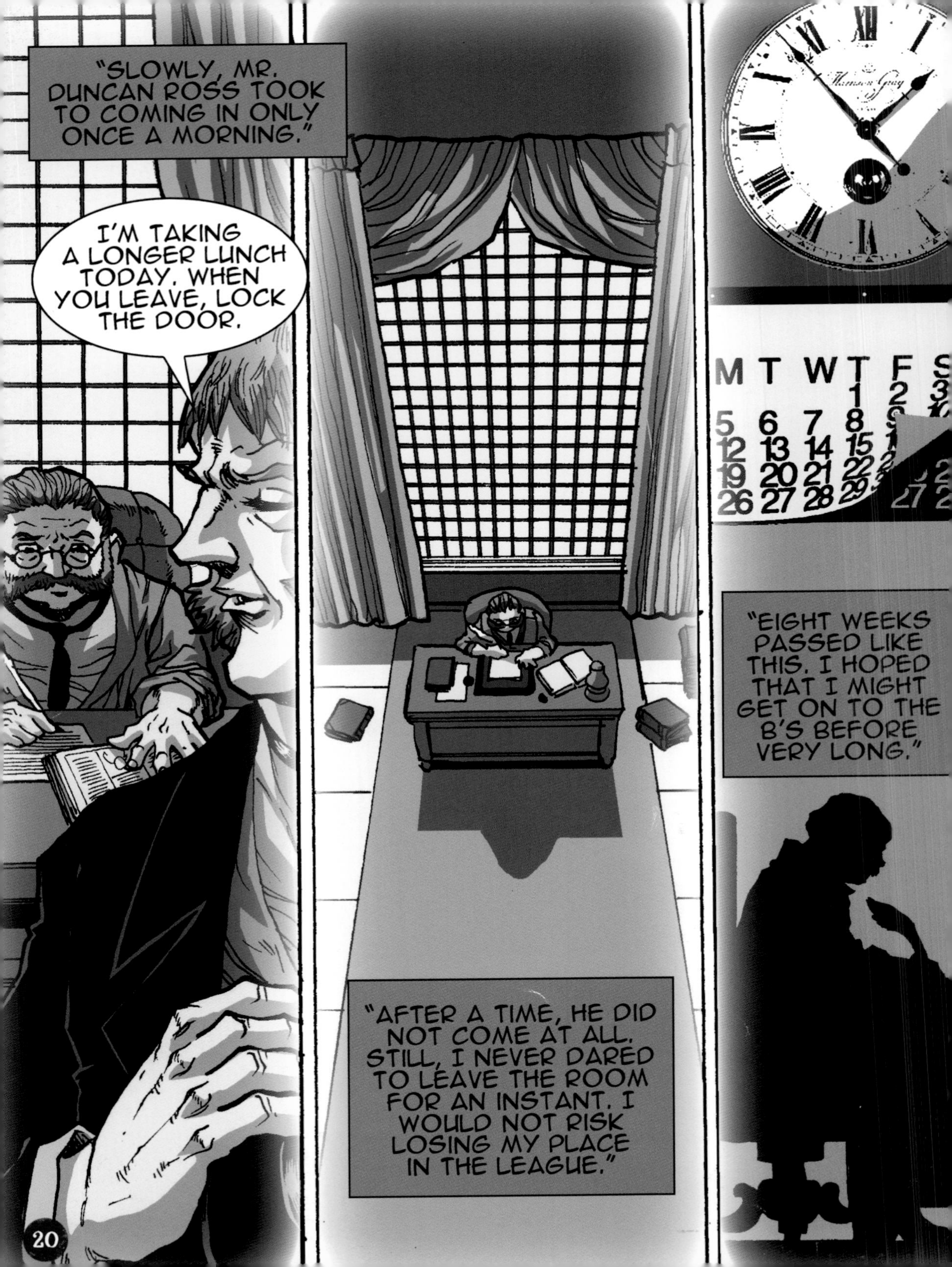

"SLOWLY, MR. DUNCAN ROSS TOOK TO COMING IN ONLY ONCE A MORNING."
I'M TAKING A LONGER LUNCH TODAY. WHEN YOU LEAVE, LOCK THE DOOR.
"AFTER A TIME, HE DID NOT COME AT ALL. STILL, I NEVER DARED TO LEAVE THE ROOM FOR AN INSTANT. I WOULD NOT RISK LOSING MY PLACE IN THE LEAGUE."
"EIGHT WEEKS PASSED LIKE THIS. I HOPED THAT I MIGHT GET ON TO THE B'S BEFORE VERY LONG."

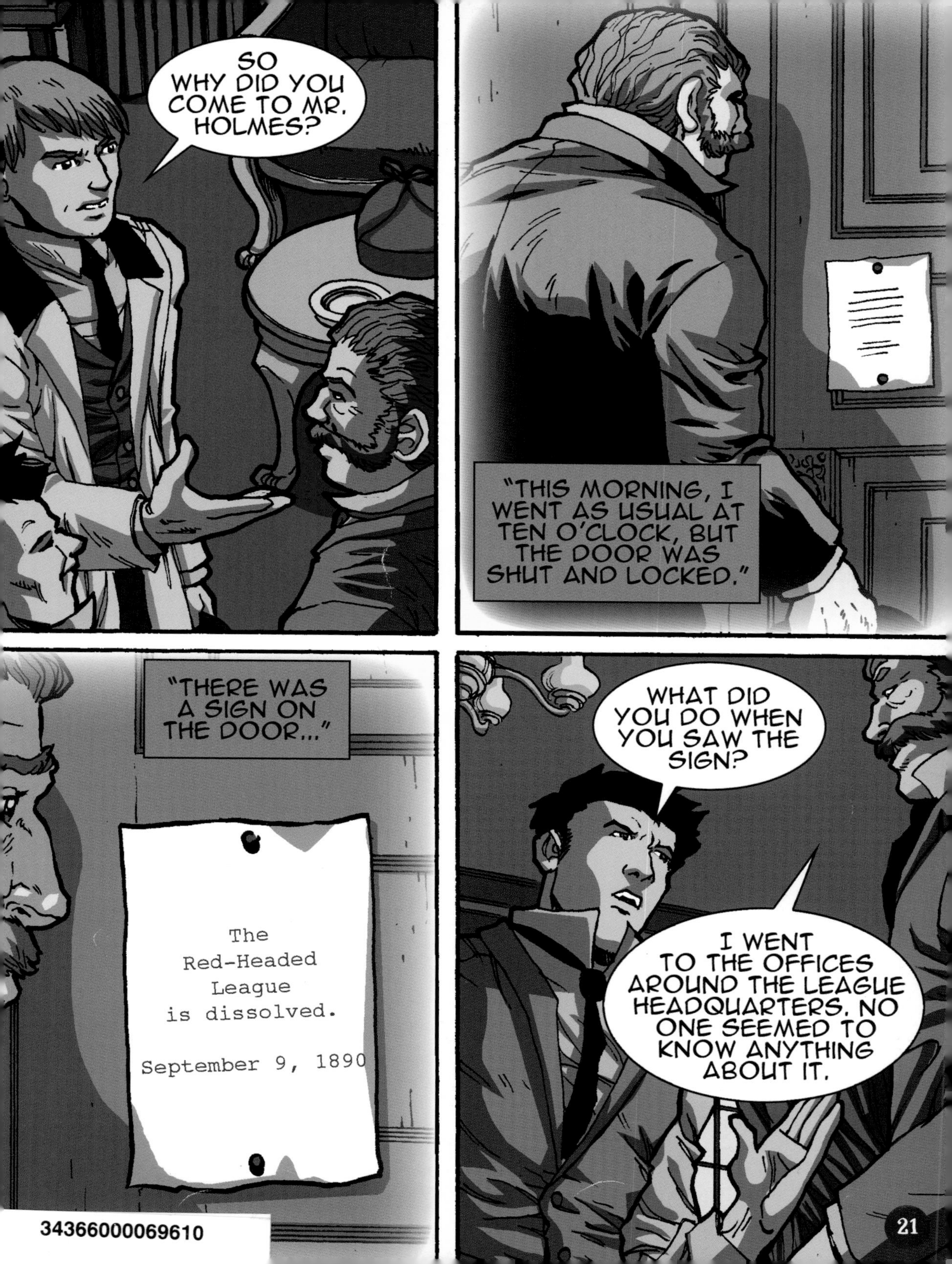

SO WHY DID YOU COME TO MR. HOLMES?
"THIS MORNING, I WENT AS USUAL AT TEN O'CLOCK, BUT THE DOOR WAS SHUT AND LOCKED."
"THERE WAS A SIGN ON THE DOOR..."
The Red-Headed League is dissolved.
September 9, 1890
WHAT DID YOU DO WHEN YOU SAW THE SIGN?
I WENT TO THE OFFICES AROUND THE LEAGUE HEADQUARTERS. NO ONE SEEMED TO KNOW ANYTHING ABOUT IT.

COULD YOU TELL ME WHAT HAS BECOME OF THE RED-HEADED LEAGUE?

THE WHAT?

THE RED-HEADED LEAGUE.

I'VE NEVER HEARD OF SUCH A THING.

THE LONDON CHAPTER IS RUN BY MR. DUNCAN ROSS.

WHO?

THE GENTLEMAN AT NUMBER 4.

THE RED-HEADED MAN?

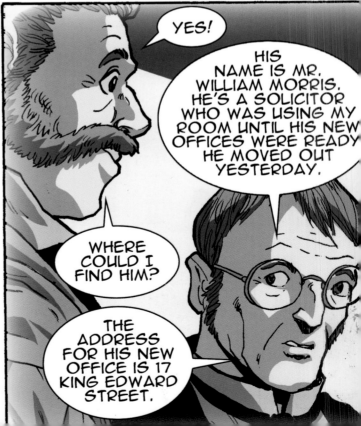

YES!

HIS NAME IS MR. WILLIAM MORRIS. HE'S A SOLICITOR WHO WAS USING MY ROOM UNTIL HIS NEW OFFICES WERE READY HE MOVED OUT YESTERDAY.

WHERE COULD I FIND HIM?

THE ADDRESS FOR HIS NEW OFFICE IS 17 KING EDWARD STREET.

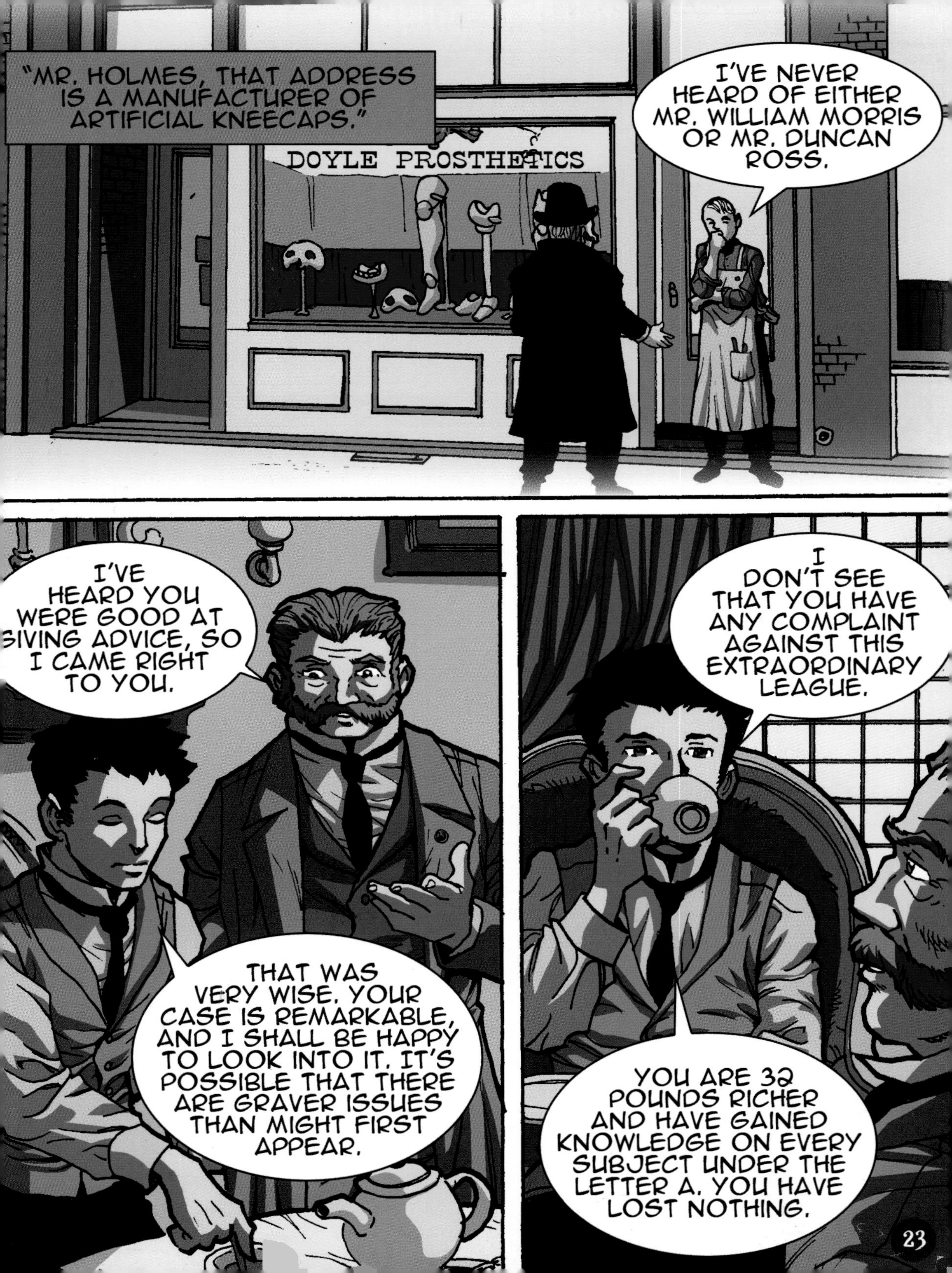
"MR. HOLMES, THAT ADDRESS IS A MANUFACTURER OF ARTIFICIAL KNEECAPS."
DOYLE PROSTHETICS
I'VE NEVER HEARD OF EITHER MR. WILLIAM MORRIS OR MR. DUNCAN ROSS.
I'VE HEARD YOU WERE GOOD AT GIVING ADVICE, SO I CAME RIGHT TO YOU.
THAT WAS VERY WISE. YOUR CASE IS REMARKABLE, AND I SHALL BE HAPPY TO LOOK INTO IT. IT'S POSSIBLE THAT THERE ARE GRAVER ISSUES THAN MIGHT FIRST APPEAR.
I DON'T SEE THAT YOU HAVE ANY COMPLAINT AGAINST THIS EXTRAORDINARY LEAGUE.
YOU ARE 32 POUNDS RICHER AND HAVE GAINED KNOWLEDGE ON EVERY SUBJECT UNDER THE LETTER A. YOU HAVE LOST NOTHING.

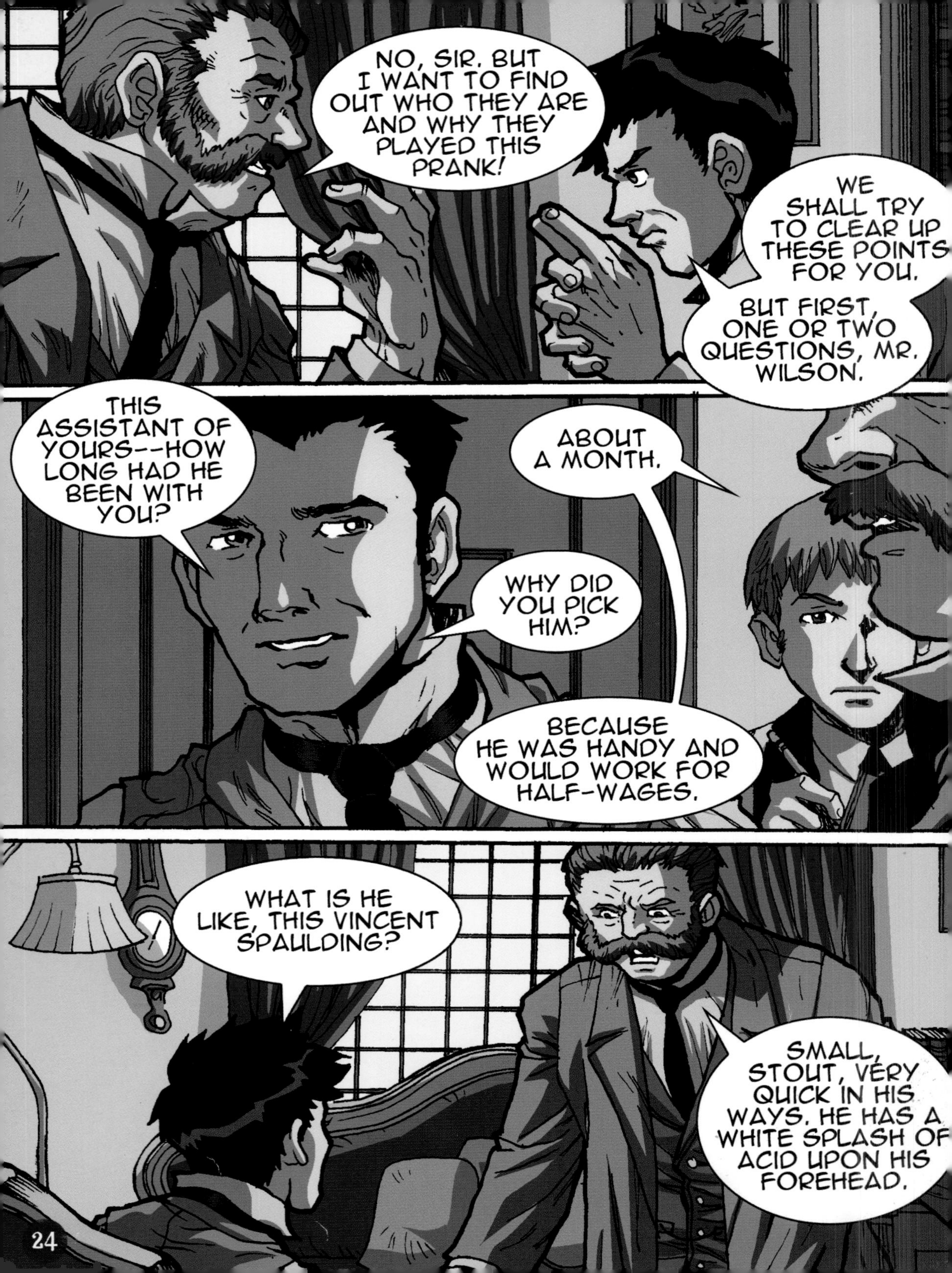
NO, SIR. BUT I WANT TO FIND OUT WHO THEY ARE AND WHY THEY PLAYED THIS PRANK!
WE SHALL TRY TO CLEAR UP THESE POINTS FOR YOU.
BUT FIRST, ONE OR TWO QUESTIONS, MR. WILSON.
THIS ASSISTANT OF YOURS--HOW LONG HAD HE BEEN WITH YOU?
ABOUT A MONTH.
WHY DID YOU PICK HIM?
BECAUSE HE WAS HANDY AND WOULD WORK FOR HALF-WAGES.
WHAT IS HE LIKE, THIS VINCENT SPAULDING?
SMALL, STOUT, VERY QUICK IN HIS WAYS. HE HAS A WHITE SPLASH OF ACID UPON HIS FOREHEAD.

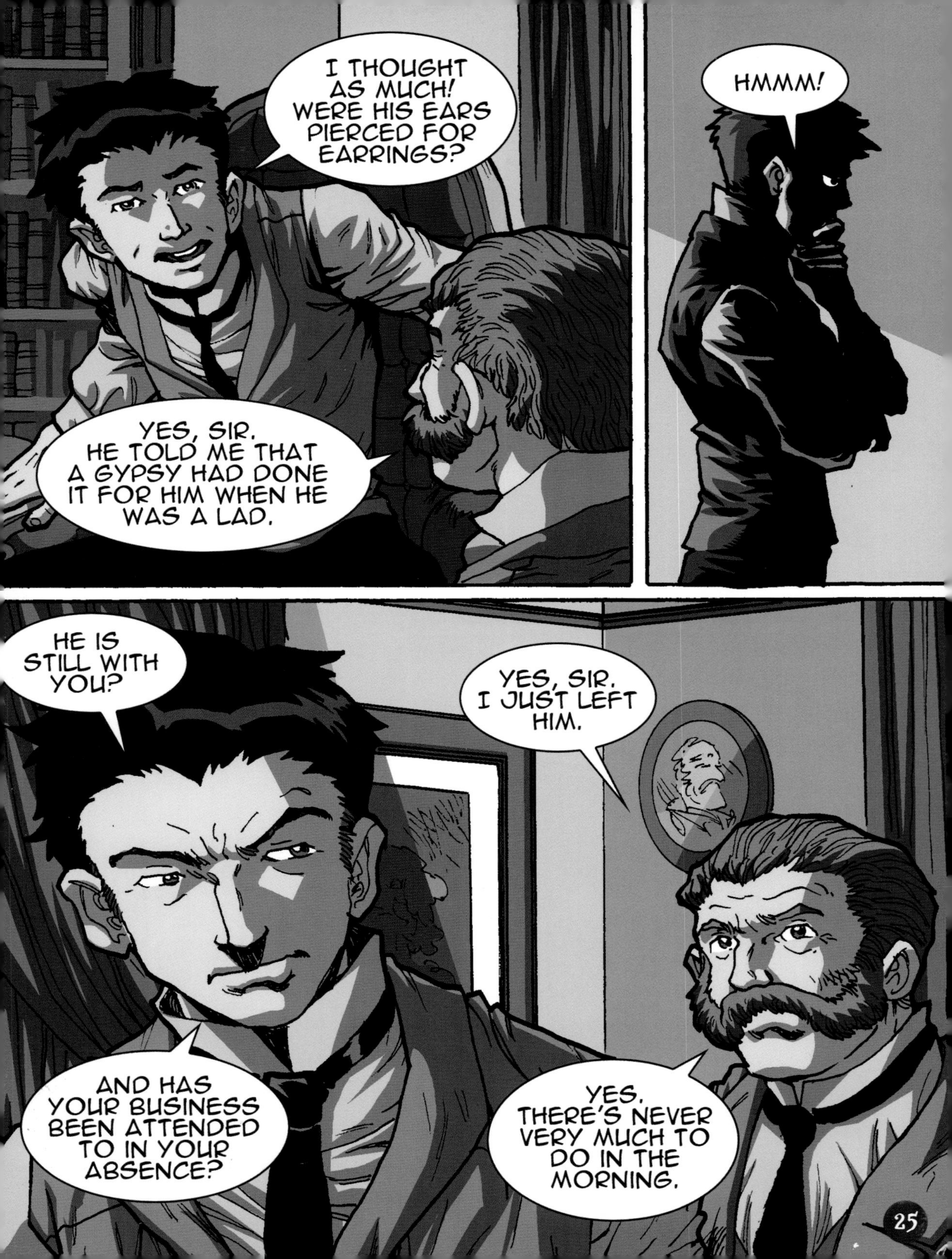
I THOUGHT AS MUCH! WERE HIS EARS PIERCED FOR EARRINGS?
YES, SIR. HE TOLD ME THAT A GYPSY HAD DONE IT FOR HIM WHEN HE WAS A LAD.
HMMM!
HE IS STILL WITH YOU?
YES, SIR. I JUST LEFT HIM.
AND HAS YOUR BUSINESS BEEN ATTENDED TO IN YOUR ABSENCE?
YES. THERE'S NEVER VERY MUCH TO DO IN THE MORNING.

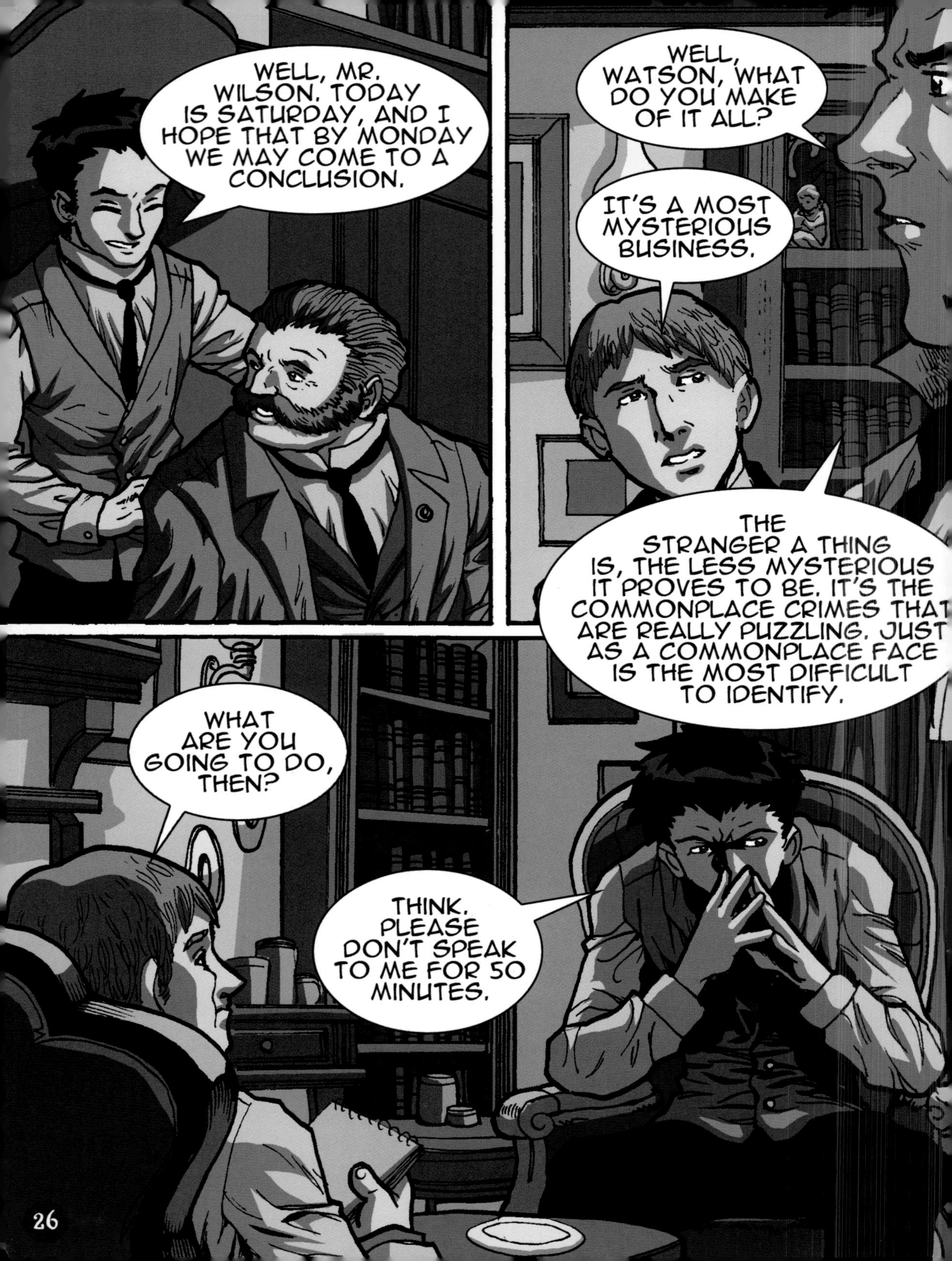
WELL, MR. WILSON. TODAY IS SATURDAY, AND I HOPE THAT BY MONDAY WE MAY COME TO A CONCLUSION.
WELL, WATSON, WHAT DO YOU MAKE OF IT ALL?
IT'S A MOST MYSTERIOUS BUSINESS.
THE STRANGER A THING IS, THE LESS MYSTERIOUS IT PROVES TO BE. IT'S THE COMMONPLACE CRIMES THAT ARE REALLY PUZZLING. JUST AS A COMMONPLACE FACE IS THE MOST DIFFICULT TO IDENTIFY.
WHAT ARE YOU GOING TO DO, THEN?
THINK. PLEASE DON'T SPEAK TO ME FOR 50 MINUTES.

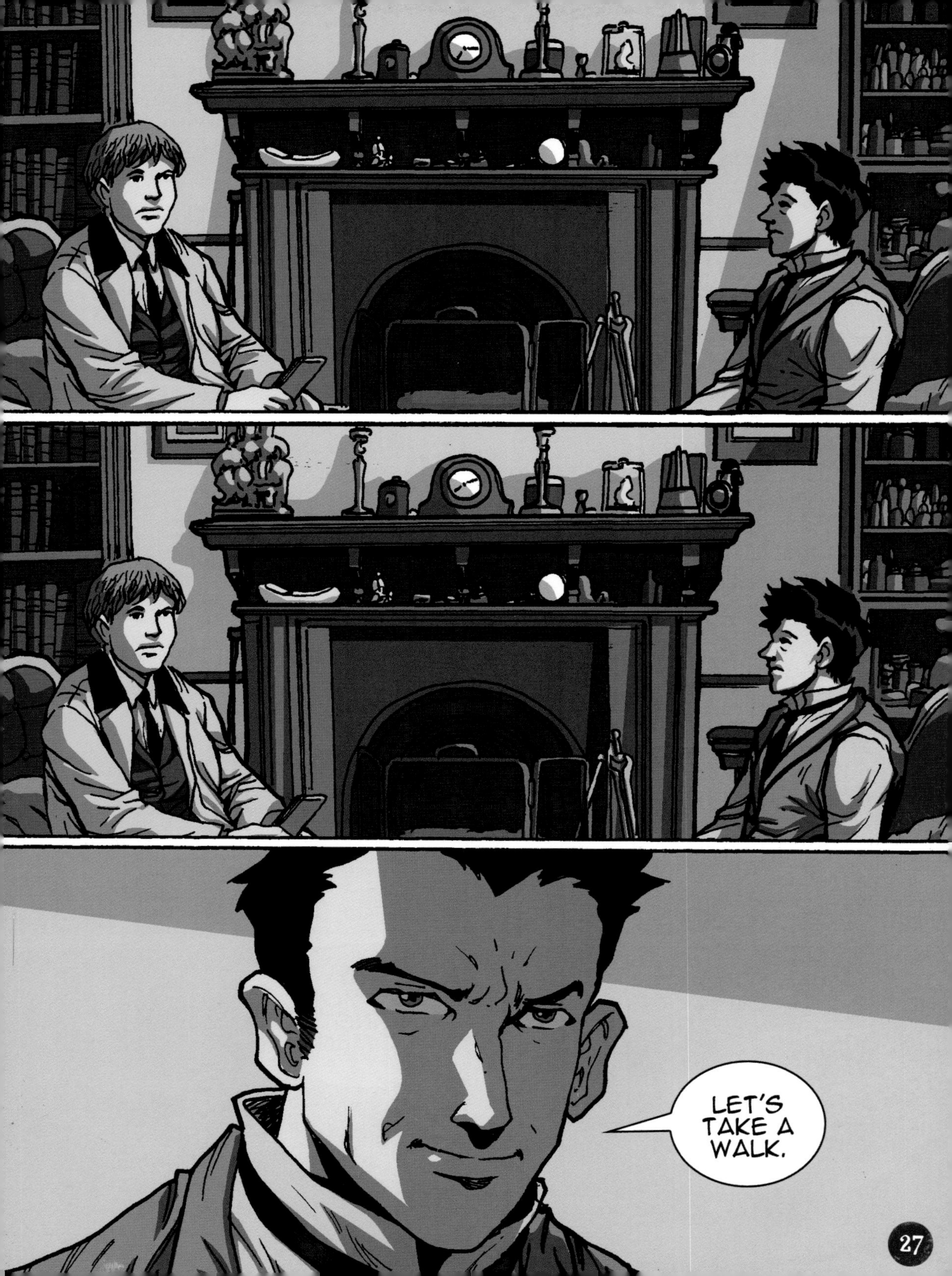
LET'S TAKE A WALK.

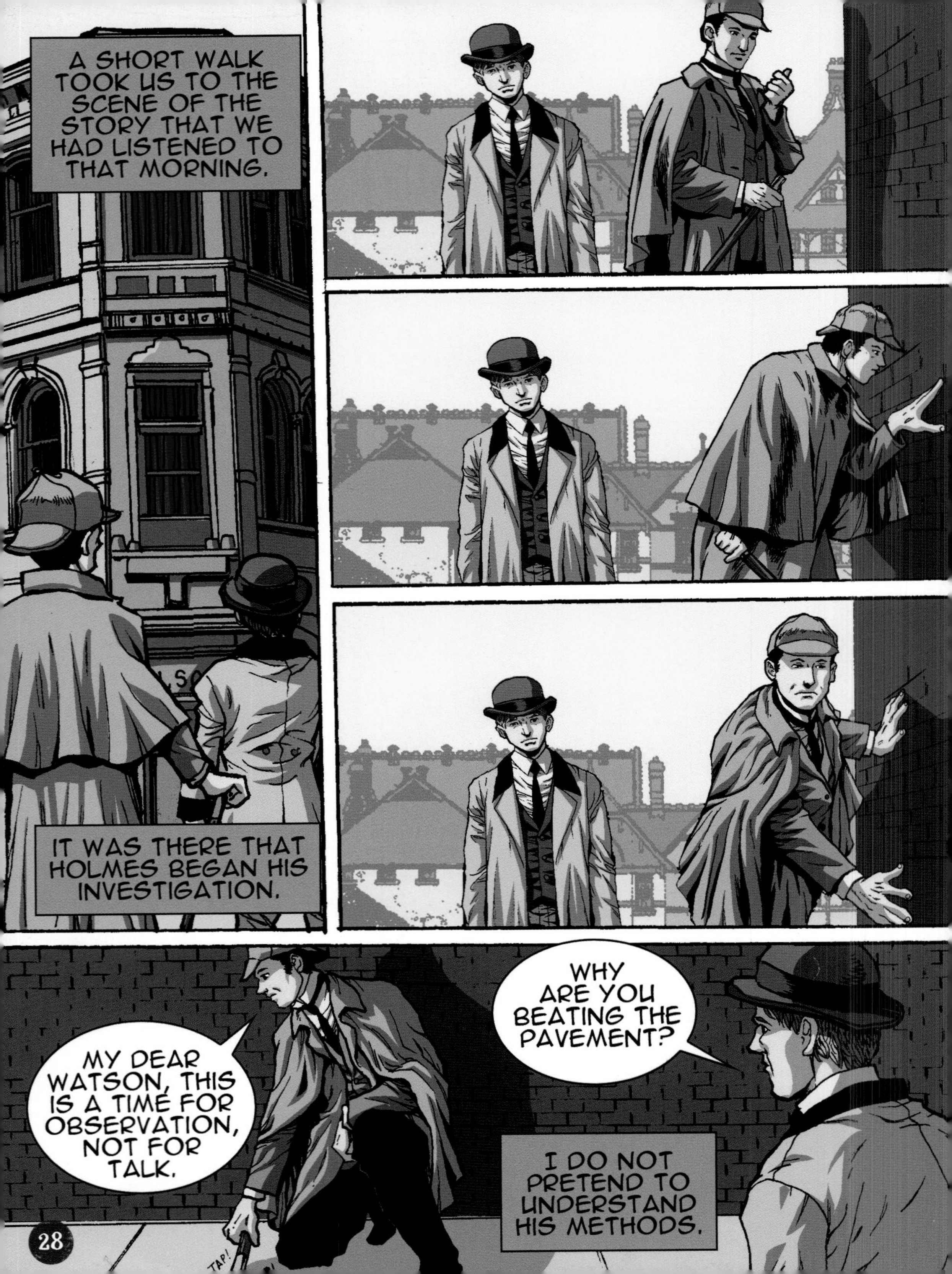
A SHORT WALK TOOK US TO THE SCENE OF THE STORY THAT WE HAD LISTENED TO THAT MORNING.
IT WAS THERE THAT HOLMES BEGAN HIS INVESTIGATION.
WHY ARE YOU BEATING THE PAVEMENT?
MY DEAR WATSON, THIS IS A TIME FOR OBSERVATION, NOT FOR TALK.
TAP!
I DO NOT PRETEND TO UNDERSTAND HIS METHODS.

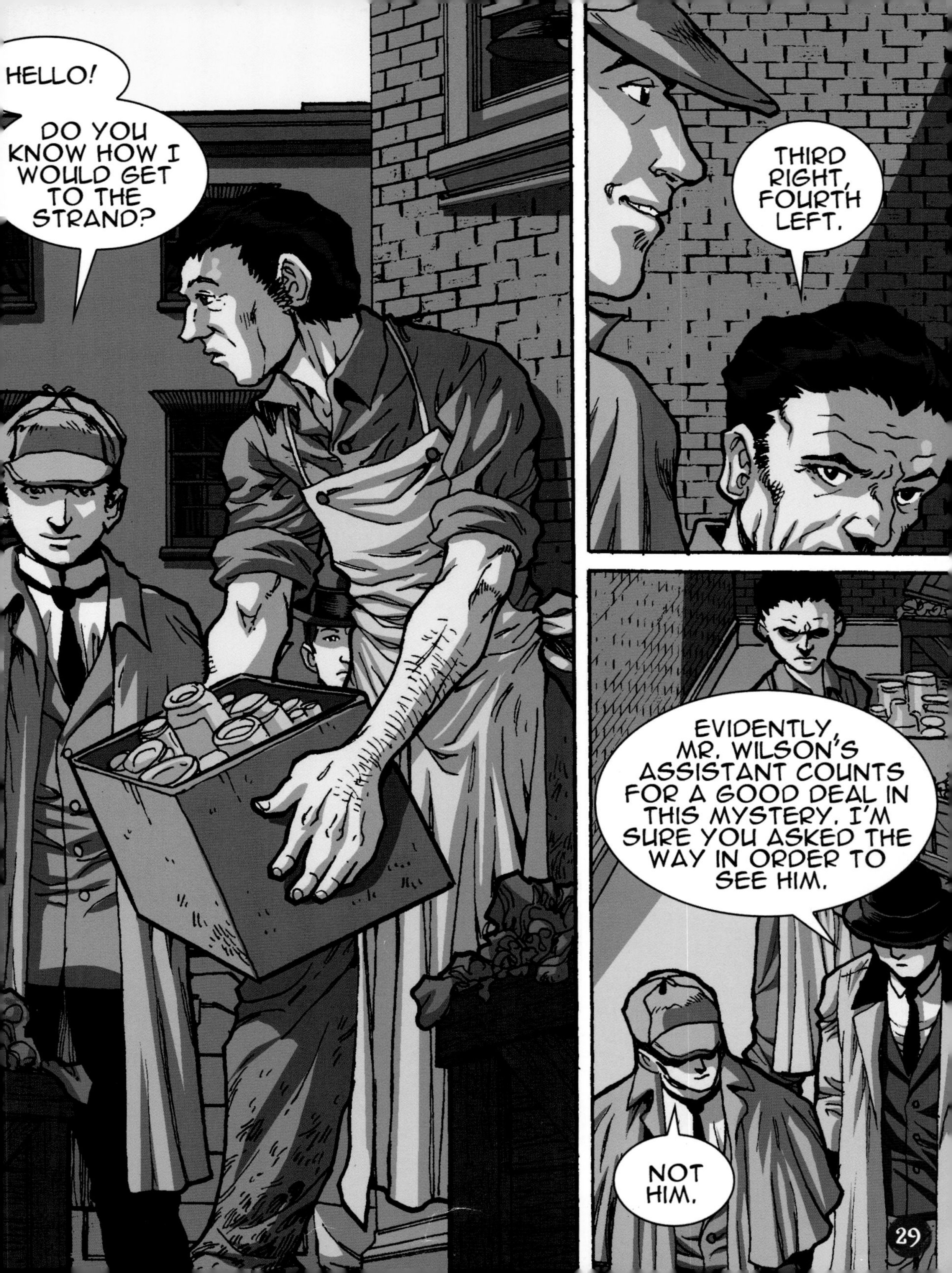
HELLO!
DO YOU KNOW HOW I WOULD GET TO THE STRAND?
THIRD RIGHT, FOURTH LEFT.
EVIDENTLY, MR. WILSON'S ASSISTANT COUNTS FOR A GOOD DEAL IN THIS MYSTERY. I'M SURE YOU ASKED THE WAY IN ORDER TO SEE HIM.
NOT HIM.

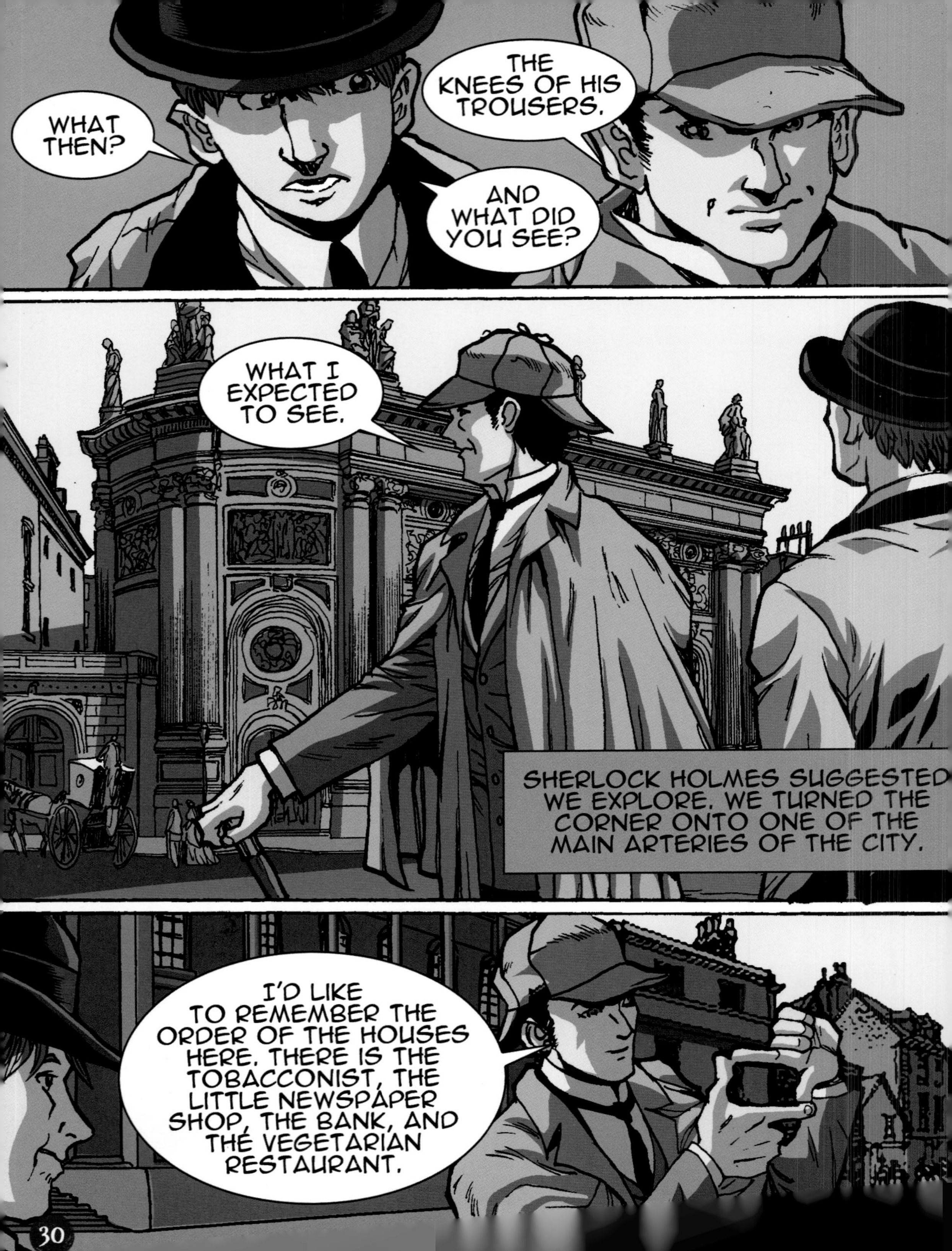
WHAT THEN?
THE KNEES OF HIS TROUSERS.
AND WHAT DID YOU SEE?
WHAT I EXPECTED TO SEE.
SHERLOCK HOLMES SUGGESTED WE EXPLORE. WE TURNED THE CORNER ONTO ONE OF THE MAIN ARTERIES OF THE CITY.
I'D LIKE TO REMEMBER THE ORDER OF THE HOUSES HERE. THERE IS THE TOBACCONIST, THE LITTLE NEWSPAPER SHOP, THE BANK, AND THE VEGETARIAN RESTAURANT.

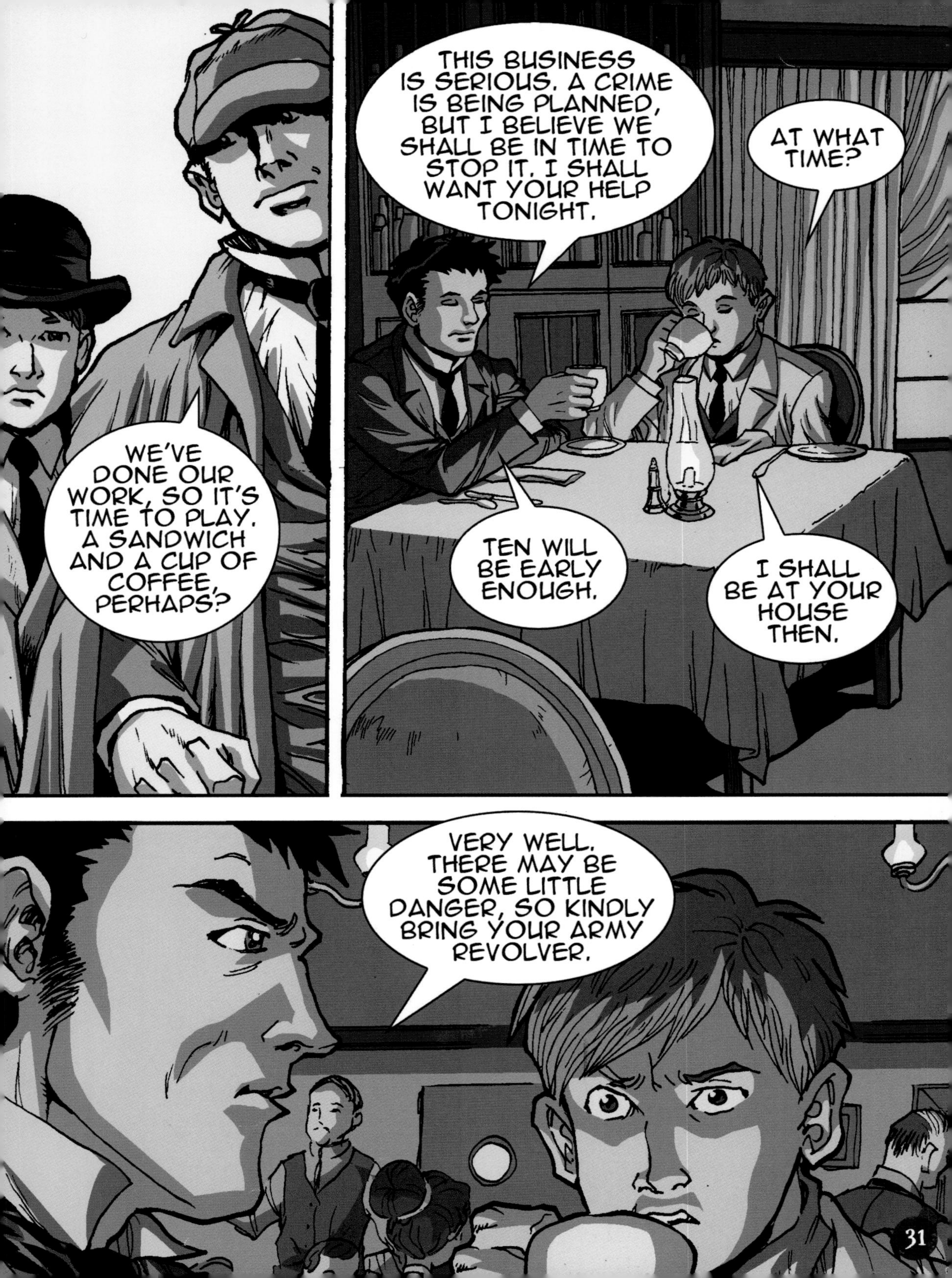
WE'VE DONE OUR WORK, SO IT'S TIME TO PLAY. A SANDWICH AND A CUP OF COFFEE, PERHAPS?
THIS BUSINESS IS SERIOUS. A CRIME IS BEING PLANNED, BUT I BELIEVE WE SHALL BE IN TIME TO STOP IT. I SHALL WANT YOUR HELP TONIGHT.
AT WHAT TIME?
TEN WILL BE EARLY ENOUGH.
I SHALL BE AT YOUR HOUSE THEN.
VERY WELL. THERE MAY BE SOME LITTLE DANGER, SO KINDLY BRING YOUR ARMY REVOLVER.

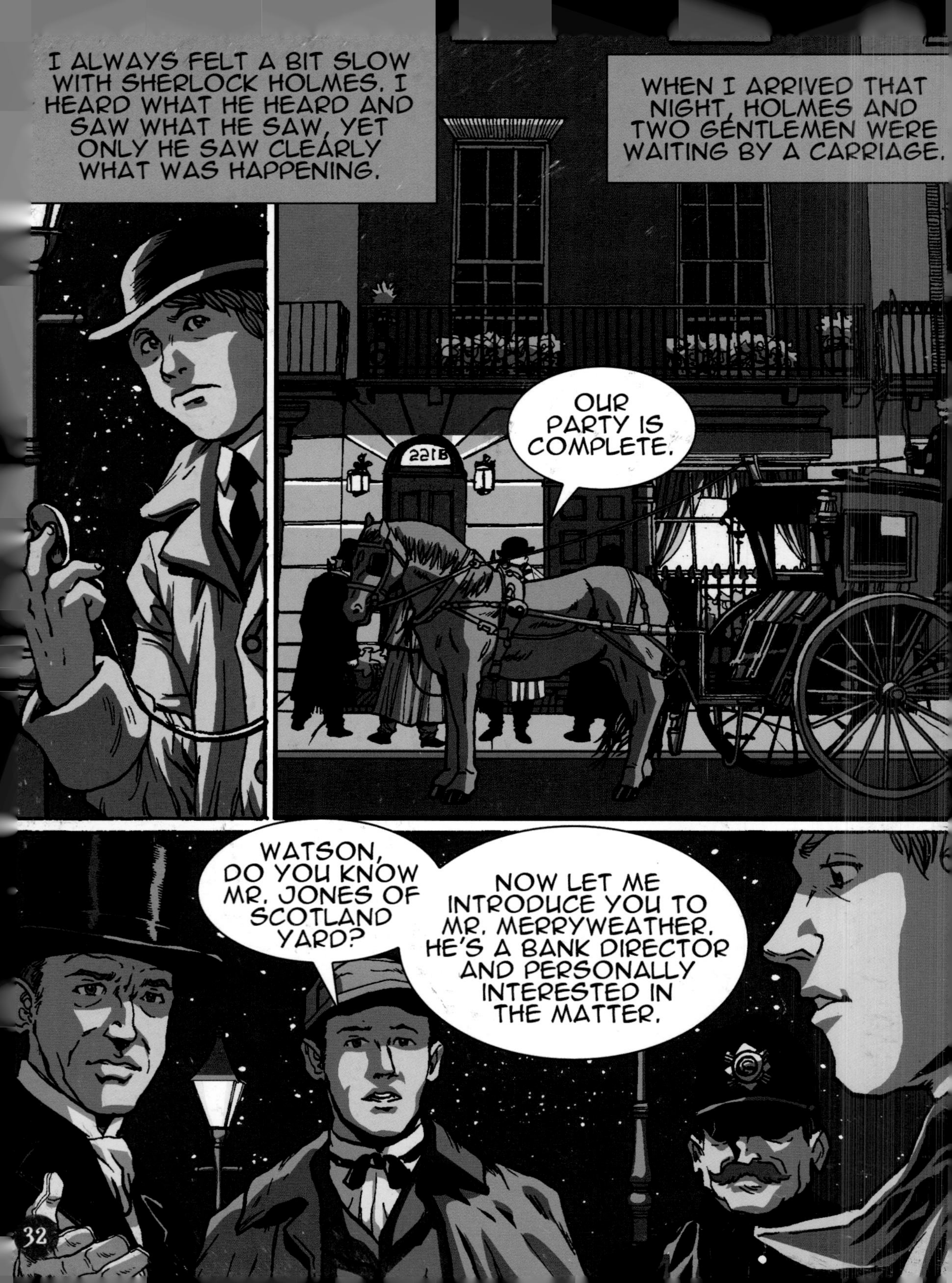

I ALWAYS FELT A BIT SLOW WITH SHERLOCK HOLMES. I HEARD WHAT HE HEARD AND SAW WHAT HE SAW, YET ONLY HE SAW CLEARLY WHAT WAS HAPPENING.
WHEN I ARRIVED THAT NIGHT, HOLMES AND TWO GENTLEMEN WERE WAITING BY A CARRIAGE.
221B
OUR PARTY IS COMPLETE.
WATSON, DO YOU KNOW MR. JONES OF SCOTLAND YARD?
NOW LET ME INTRODUCE YOU TO MR. MERRYWEATHER. HE'S A BANK DIRECTOR AND PERSONALLY INTERESTED IN THE MATTER.

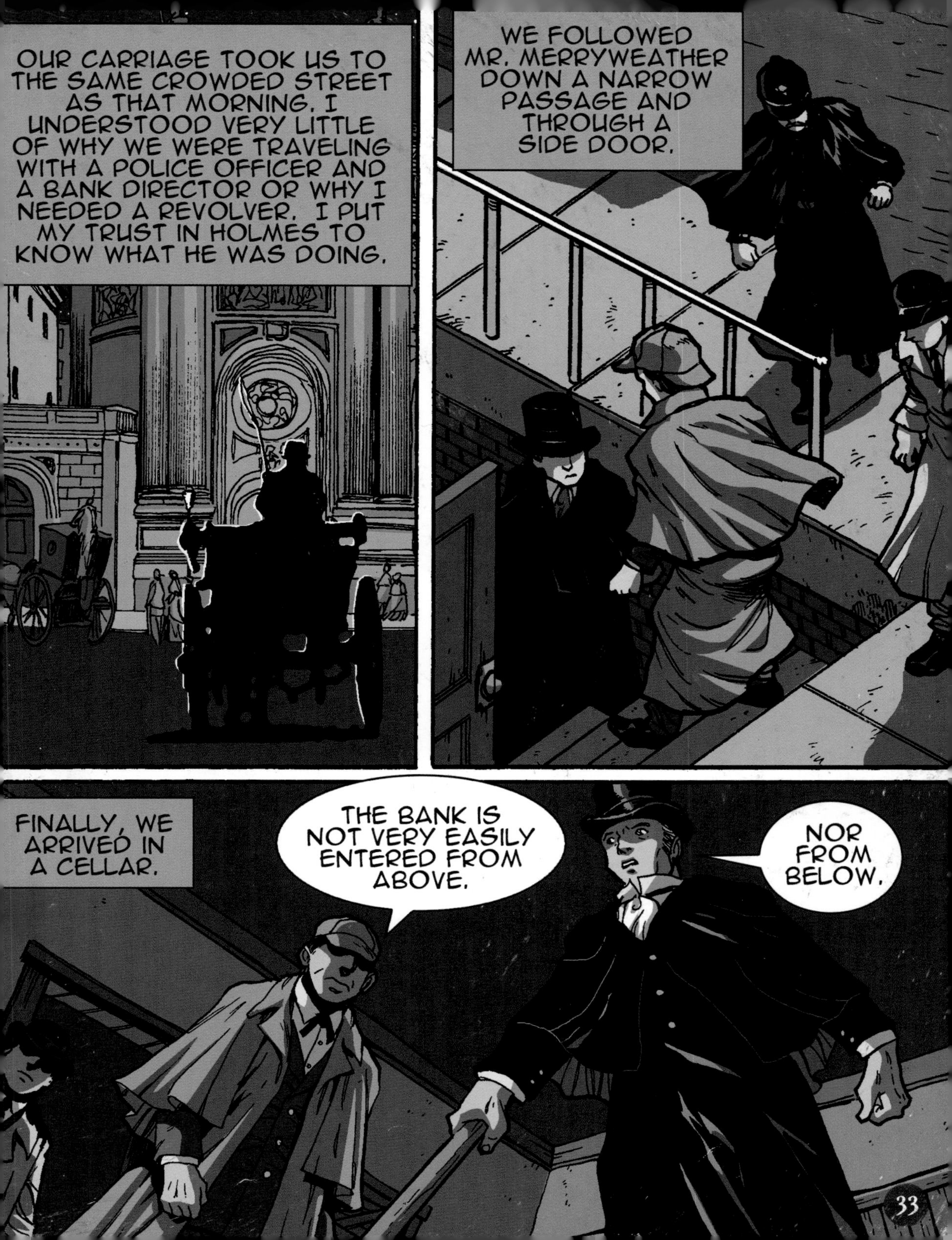
OUR CARRIAGE TOOK US TO THE SAME CROWDED STREET AS THAT MORNING. I UNDERSTOOD VERY LITTLE OF WHY WE WERE TRAVELING WITH A POLICE OFFICER AND A BANK DIRECTOR OR WHY I NEEDED A REVOLVER. I PUT MY TRUST IN HOLMES TO KNOW WHAT HE WAS DOING.
WE FOLLOWED MR. MERRYWEATHER DOWN A NARROW PASSAGE AND THROUGH A SIDE DOOR.
FINALLY, WE ARRIVED IN A CELLAR.
THE BANK IS NOT VERY EASILY ENTERED FROM ABOVE.
NOR FROM BELOW.

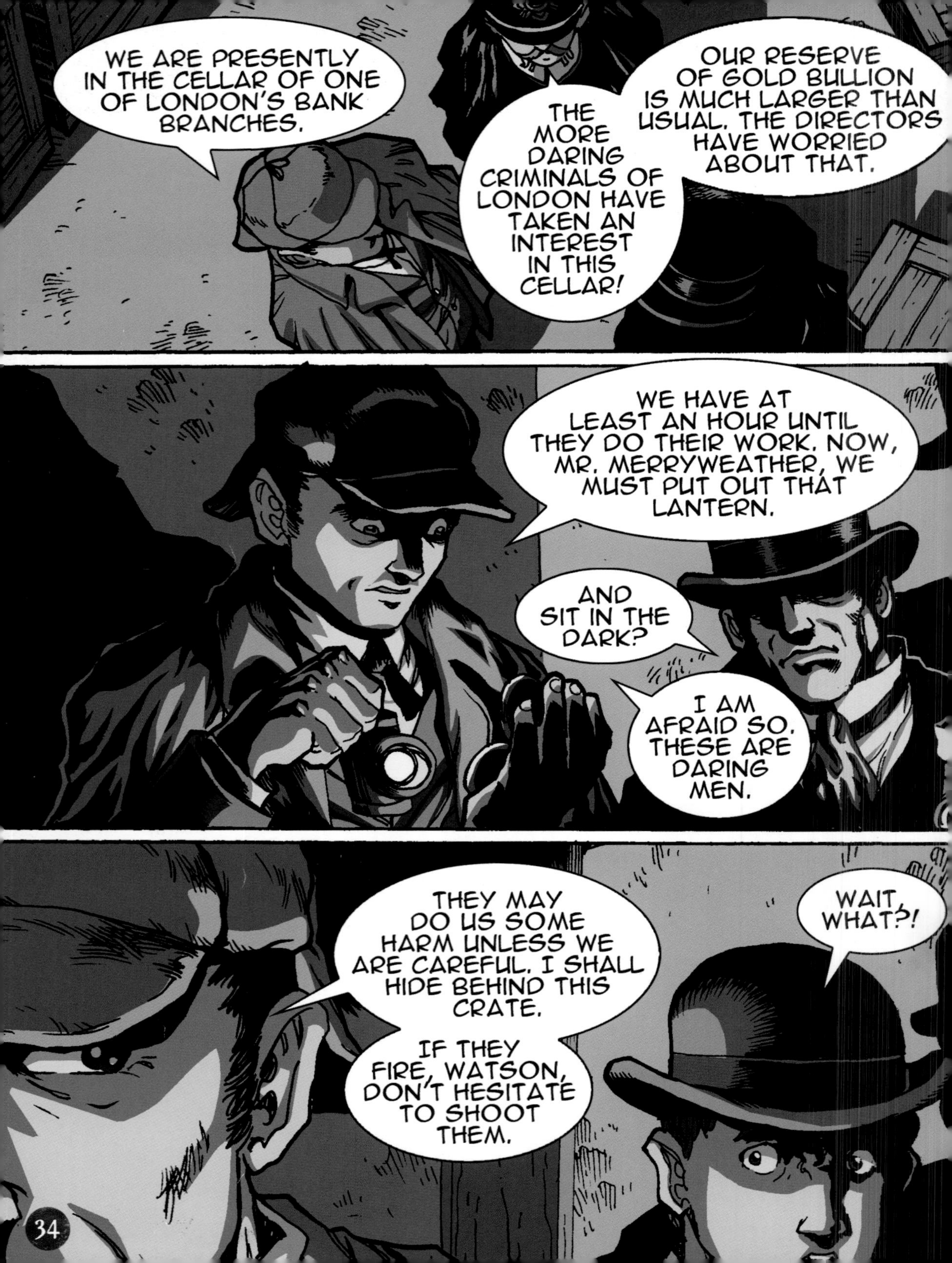
WE ARE PRESENTLY IN THE CELLAR OF ONE OF LONDON'S BANK BRANCHES.
THE MORE DARING CRIMINALS OF LONDON HAVE TAKEN AN INTEREST IN THIS CELLAR!
OUR RESERVE OF GOLD BULLION IS MUCH LARGER THAN USUAL. THE DIRECTORS HAVE WORRIED ABOUT THAT.
WE HAVE AT LEAST AN HOUR UNTIL THEY DO THEIR WORK. NOW, MR. MERRYWEATHER, WE MUST PUT OUT THAT LANTERN.
AND SIT IN THE DARK?
I AM AFRAID SO. THESE ARE DARING MEN.
THEY MAY DO US SOME HARM UNLESS WE ARE CAREFUL. I SHALL HIDE BEHIND THIS CRATE.
IF THEY FIRE, WATSON, DON'T HESITATE TO SHOOT THEM.
WAIT, WHAT?!

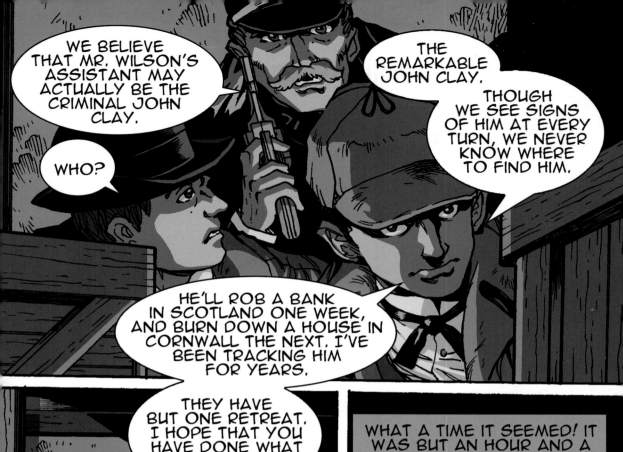

WE BELIEVE THAT MR. WILSON'S ASSISTANT MAY ACTUALLY BE THE CRIMINAL JOHN CLAY.

WHO?

THE REMARKABLE JOHN CLAY.

THOUGH WE SEE SIGNS OF HIM AT EVERY TURN, WE NEVER KNOW WHERE TO FIND HIM.

HE'LL ROB A BANK IN SCOTLAND ONE WEEK, AND BURN DOWN A HOUSE IN CORNWALL THE NEXT. I'VE BEEN TRACKING HIM FOR YEARS.

THEY HAVE BUT ONE RETREAT. I HOPE THAT YOU HAVE DONE WHAT I ASKED YOU, JONES.

I HAVE AN INSPECTOR AND TWO OFFICERS WAITING AT THE FRONT DOOR.

THEN WE HAVE STOPPED ALL THE HOLES, AND NOW WE MUST BE SILENT AND WAIT.

WHAT A TIME IT SEEMED! IT WAS BUT AN HOUR AND A QUARTER, BUT IT SEEMED THAT THE NIGHT MUST HAVE ALMOST GONE.

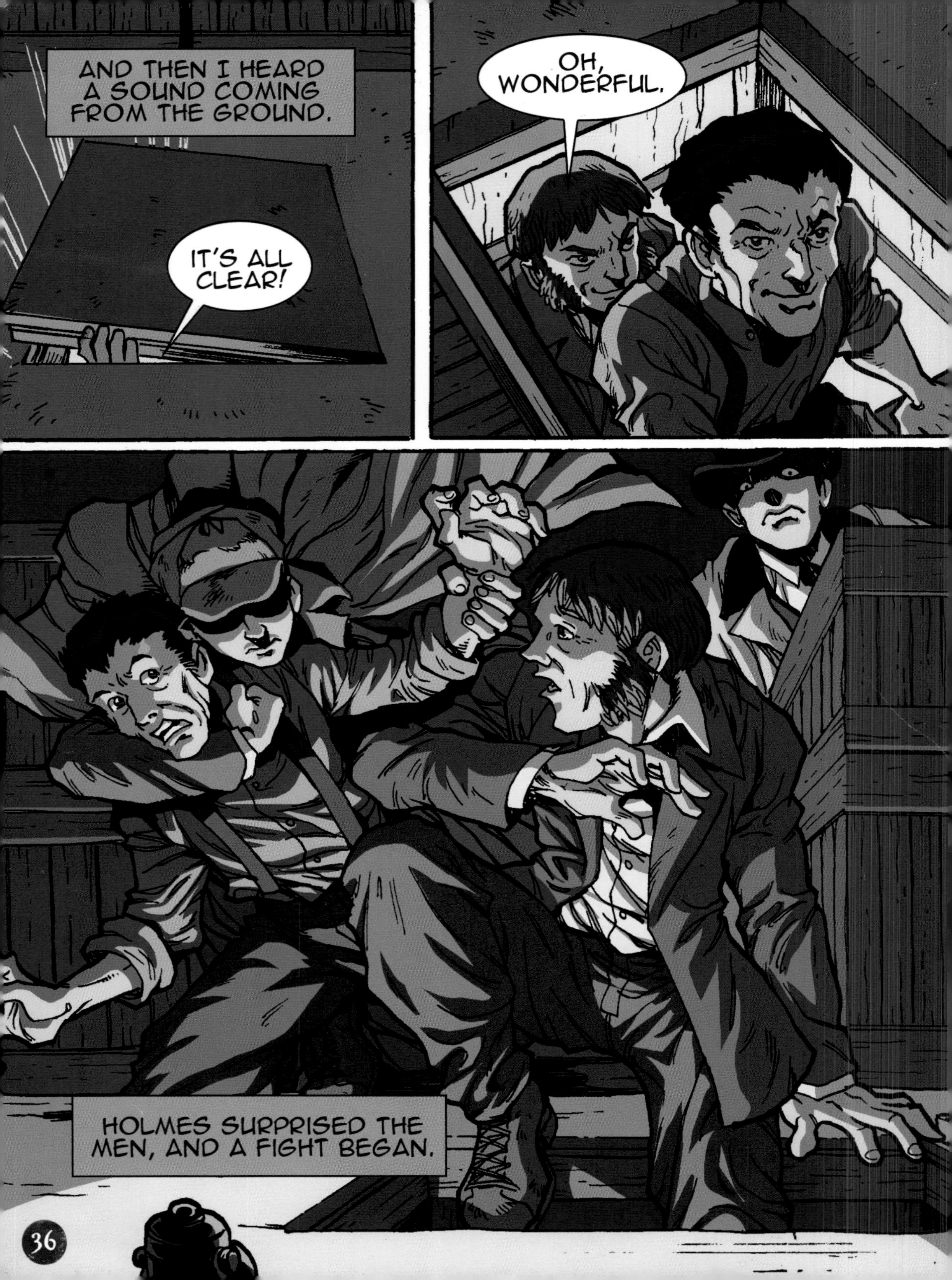
AND THEN I HEARD A SOUND COMING FROM THE GROUND.
IT'S ALL CLEAR!
OH, WONDERFUL.
HOLMES SURPRISED THE MEN, AND A FIGHT BEGAN.

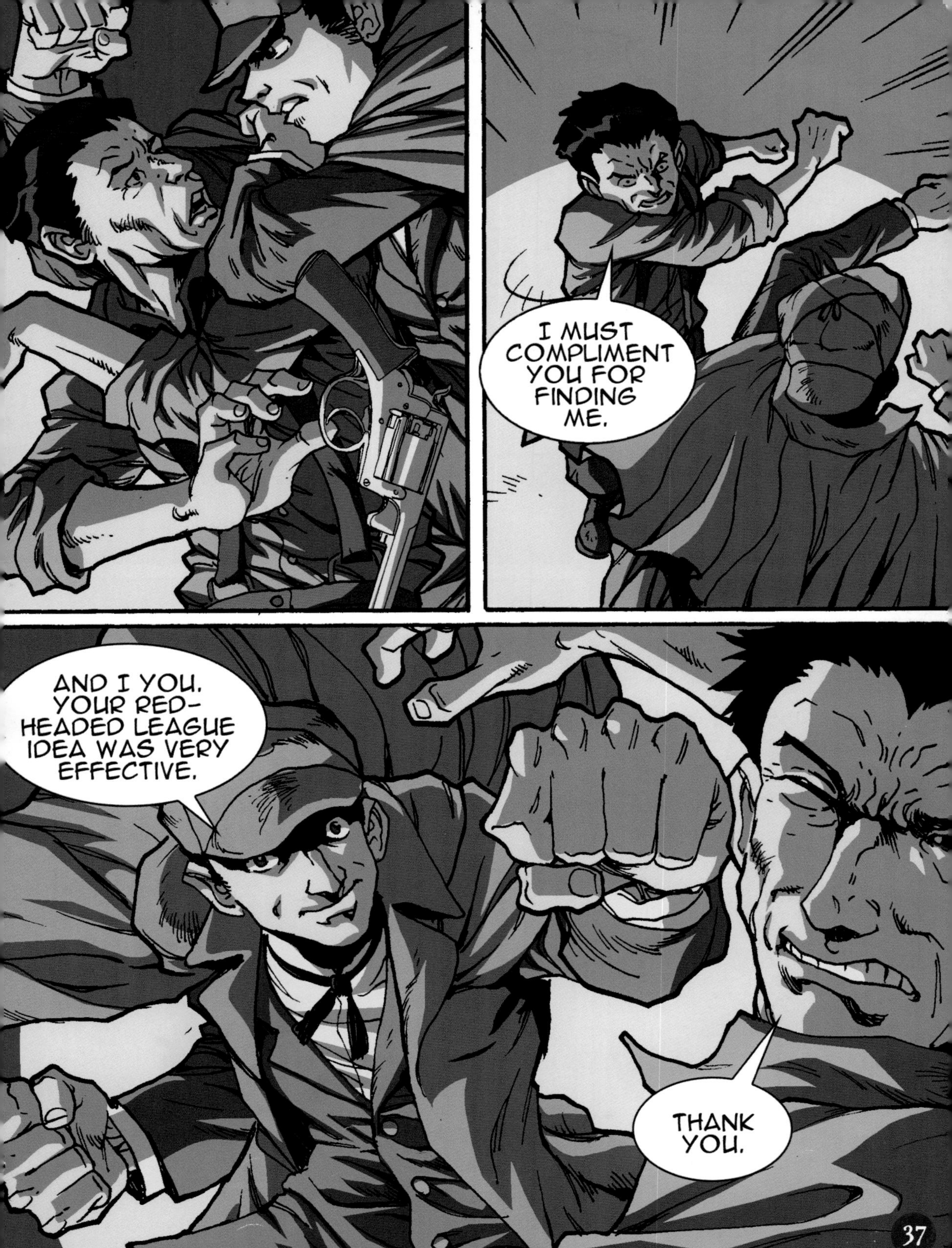
I MUST COMPLIMENT YOU FOR FINDING ME.
AND I YOU. YOUR RED-HEADED LEAGUE IDEA WAS VERY EFFECTIVE.
THANK YOU.

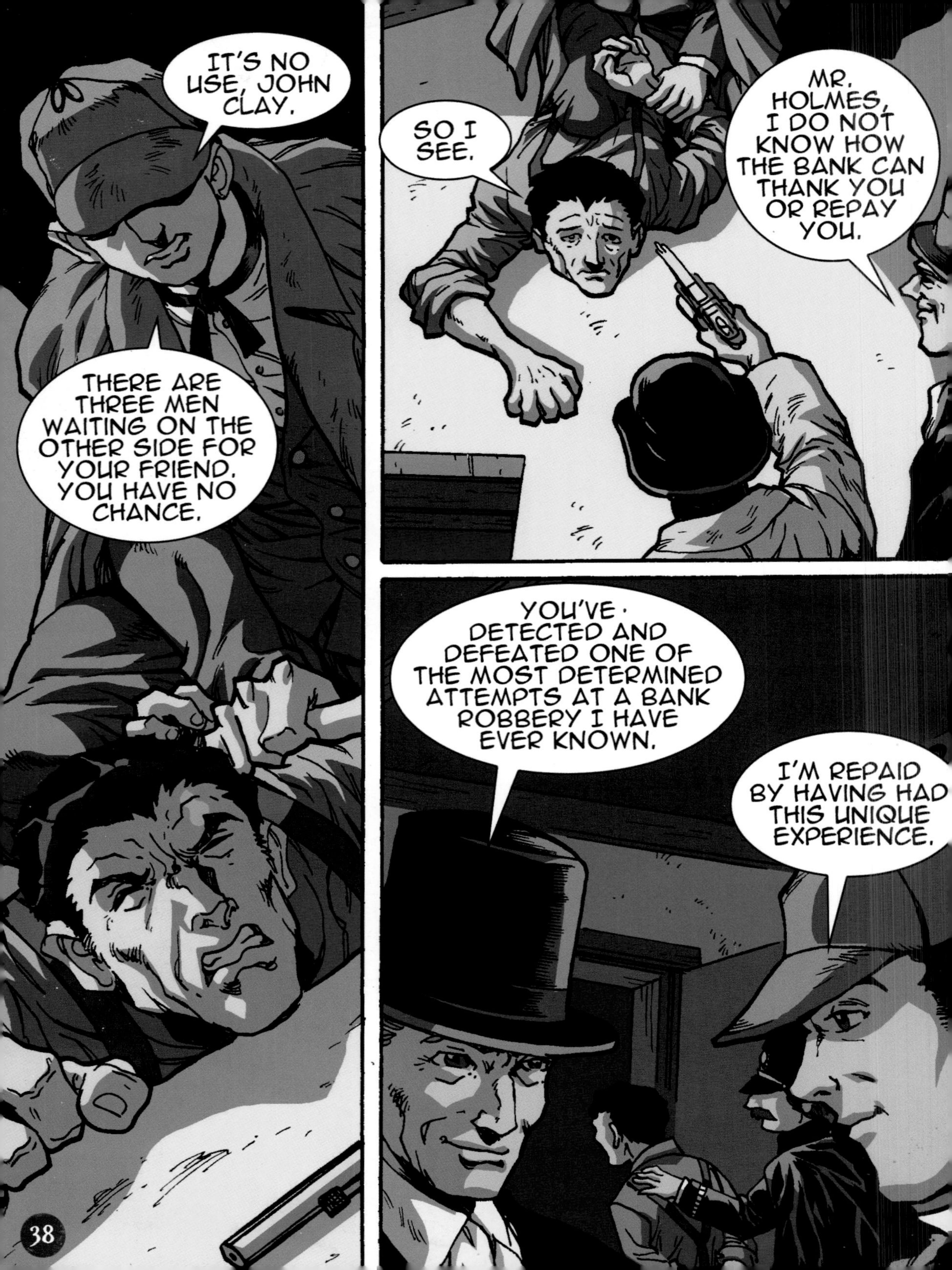

IT'S NO USE, JOHN CLAY.
THERE ARE THREE MEN WAITING ON THE OTHER SIDE FOR YOUR FRIEND. YOU HAVE NO CHANCE.
SO I SEE.
MR. HOLMES, I DO NOT KNOW HOW THE BANK CAN THANK YOU OR REPAY YOU.
YOU'VE DETECTED AND DEFEATED ONE OF THE MOST DETERMINED ATTEMPTS AT A BANK ROBBERY I HAVE EVER KNOWN.
I'M REPAID BY HAVING HAD THIS UNIQUE EXPERIENCE.

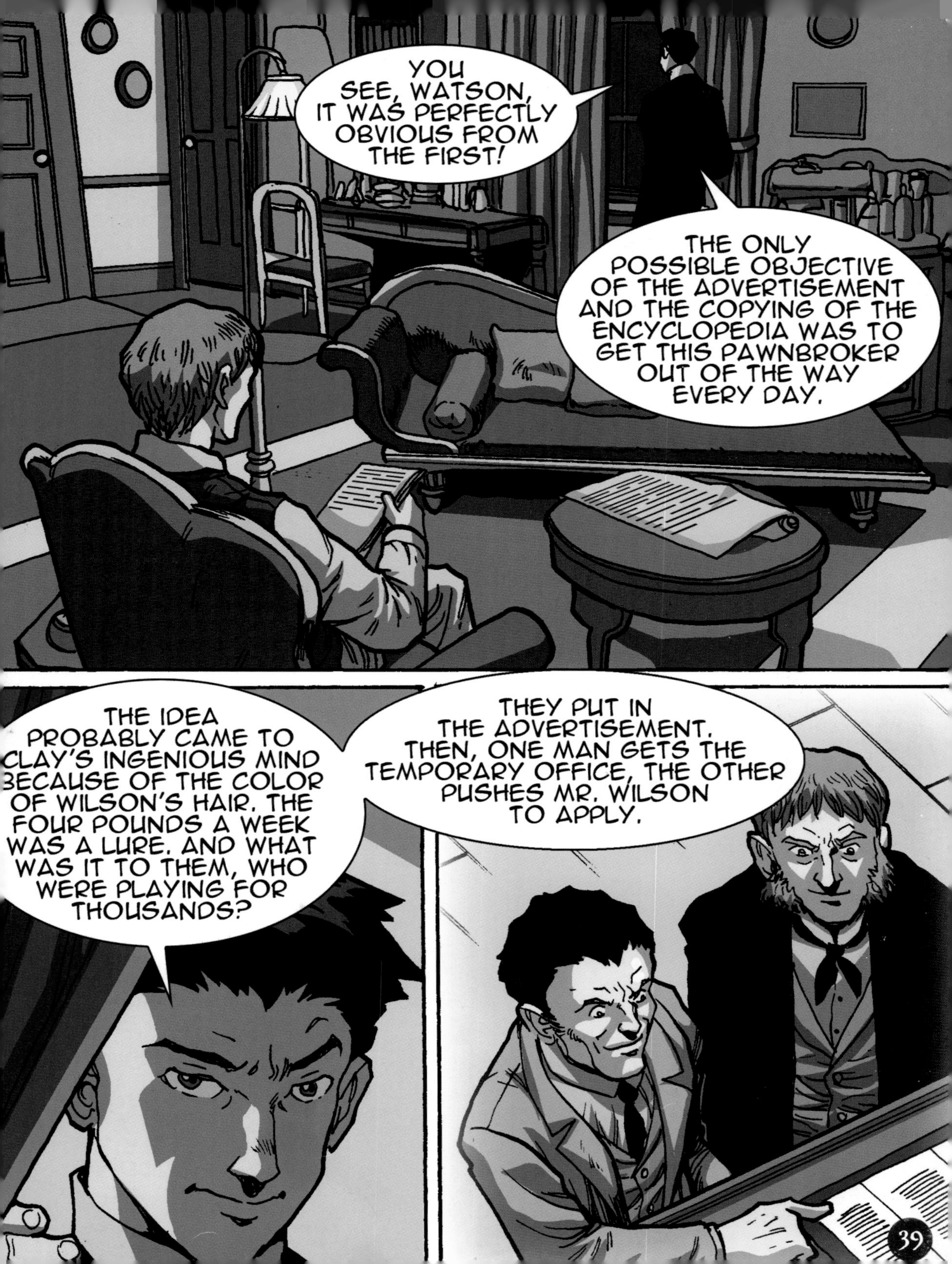
YOU SEE, WATSON, IT WAS PERFECTLY OBVIOUS FROM THE FIRST!
THE ONLY POSSIBLE OBJECTIVE OF THE ADVERTISEMENT AND THE COPYING OF THE ENCYCLOPEDIA WAS TO GET THIS PAWNBROKER OUT OF THE WAY EVERY DAY.
THE IDEA PROBABLY CAME TO CLAY'S INGENIOUS MIND BECAUSE OF THE COLOR OF WILSON'S HAIR. THE FOUR POUNDS A WEEK WAS A LURE. AND WHAT WAS IT TO THEM, WHO WERE PLAYING FOR THOUSANDS?
THEY PUT IN THE ADVERTISEMENT. THEN, ONE MAN GETS THE TEMPORARY OFFICE, THE OTHER PUSHES MR. WILSON TO APPLY.

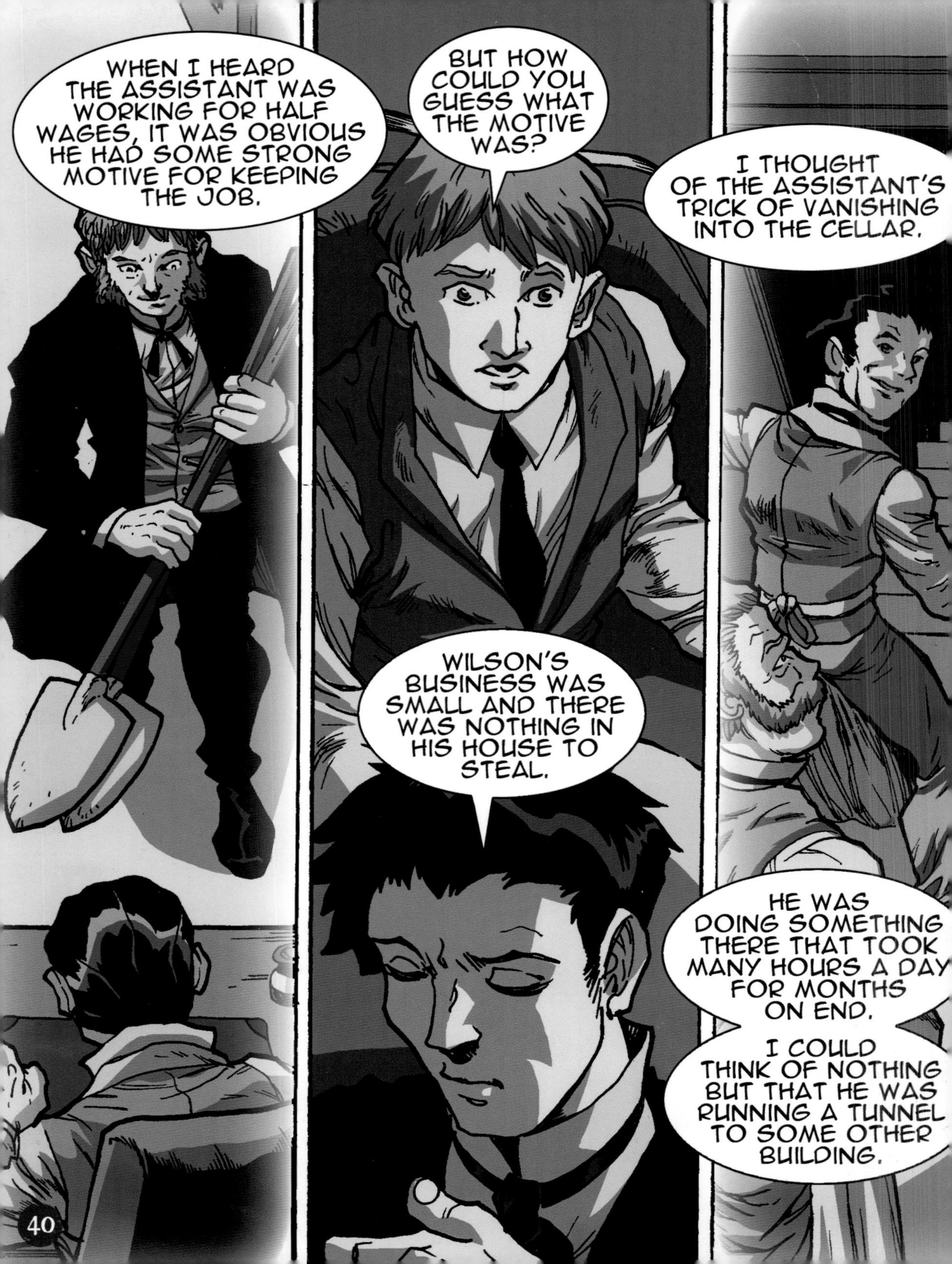
WHEN I HEARD THE ASSISTANT WAS WORKING FOR HALF WAGES, IT WAS OBVIOUS HE HAD SOME STRONG MOTIVE FOR KEEPING THE JOB.
BUT HOW COULD YOU GUESS WHAT THE MOTIVE WAS?
WILSON'S BUSINESS WAS SMALL AND THERE WAS NOTHING IN HIS HOUSE TO STEAL.
I THOUGHT OF THE ASSISTANT'S TRICK OF VANISHING INTO THE CELLAR.
HE WAS DOING SOMETHING THERE THAT TOOK MANY HOURS A DAY FOR MONTHS ON END.
I COULD THINK OF NOTHING BUT THAT HE WAS RUNNING A TUNNEL TO SOME OTHER BUILDING.

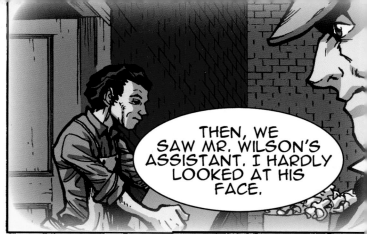

WHEN WE WENT TO THE SCENE, I SURPRISED YOU BY BEATING THE GROUND WITH MY STICK. I WAS CHECKING TO SEE IF THE CELLAR STRETCHED OUT IN FRONT OR BEHIND. IT WAS NOT IN FRONT.

THEN, WE SAW MR. WILSON'S ASSISTANT. I HARDLY LOOKED AT HIS FACE.

TAP! TAP! TAP!

HIS KNEES WERE WHAT I WISHED TO SEE. YOU MUST YOURSELF HAVE REMARKED HOW STAINED THEY WERE.

I WALKED 'ROUND THE CORNER AND SAW THE BANK WAS NEXT TO OUR FRIEND'S BUSINESS! THAT'S WHEN I FELT THAT I HAD SOLVED THE CASE.

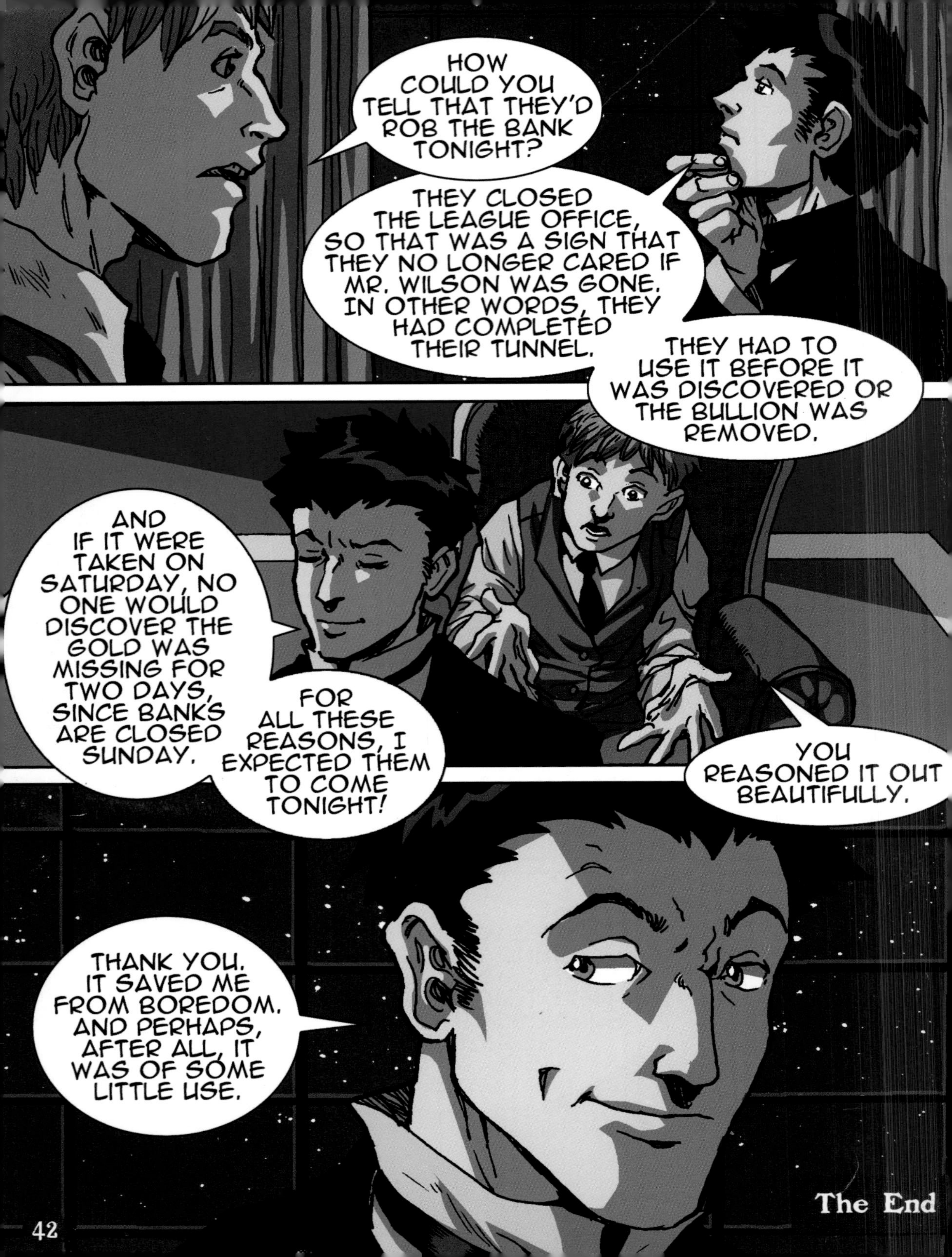
HOW COULD YOU TELL THAT THEY'D ROB THE BANK TONIGHT?
THEY CLOSED THE LEAGUE OFFICE, SO THAT WAS A SIGN THAT THEY NO LONGER CARED IF MR. WILSON WAS GONE. IN OTHER WORDS, THEY HAD COMPLETED THEIR TUNNEL.
THEY HAD TO USE IT BEFORE IT WAS DISCOVERED OR THE BULLION WAS REMOVED.
AND IF IT WERE TAKEN ON SATURDAY, NO ONE WOULD DISCOVER THE GOLD WAS MISSING FOR TWO DAYS, SINCE BANKS ARE CLOSED SUNDAY.
FOR ALL THESE REASONS, I EXPECTED THEM TO COME TONIGHT!
YOU REASONED IT OUT BEAUTIFULLY.
THANK YOU. IT SAVED ME FROM BOREDOM. AND PERHAPS, AFTER ALL, IT WAS OF SOME LITTLE USE.

The End

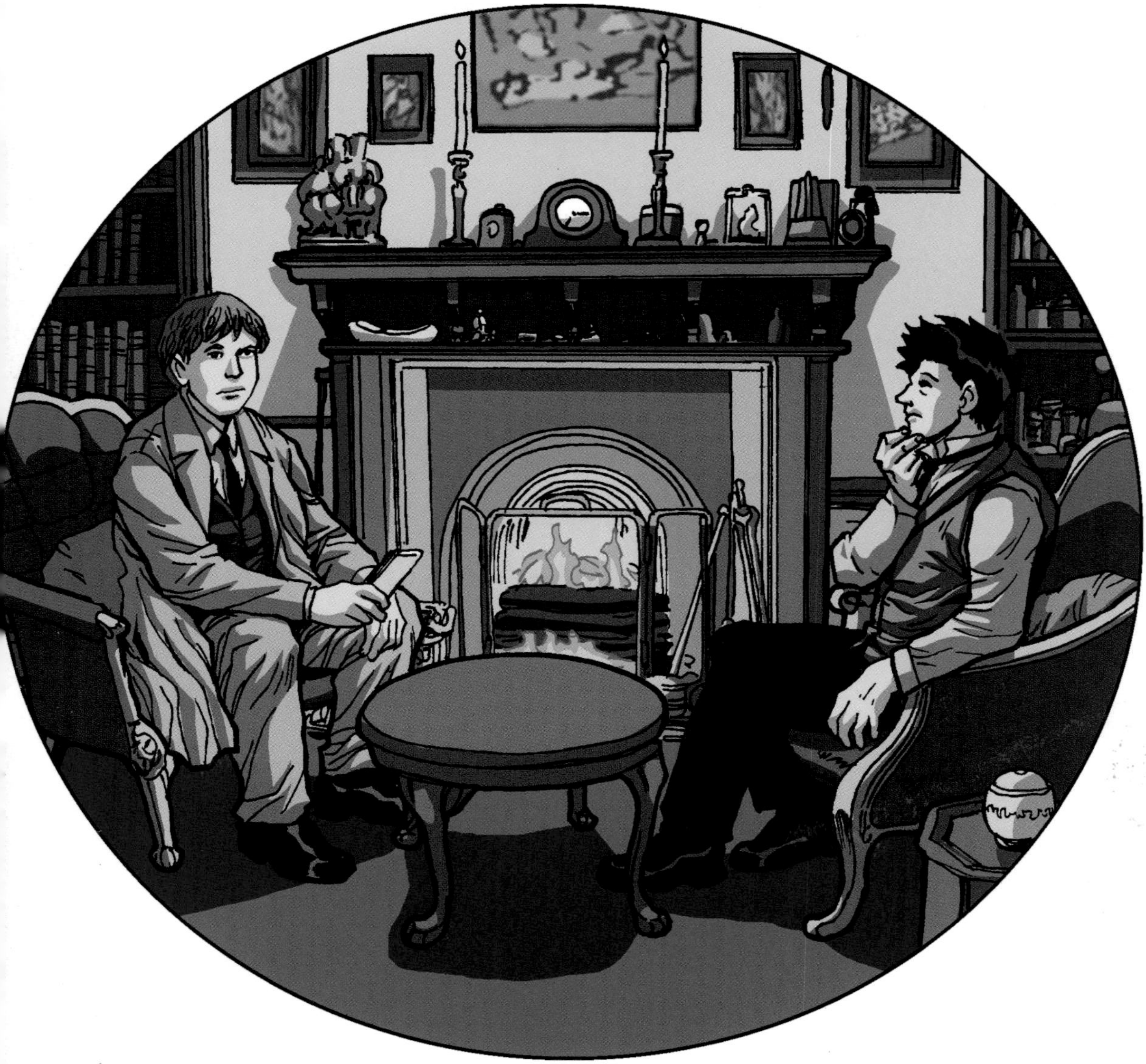

How to Draw
Sherlock Holmes
by Ben Dunn

Step 1: Use a pencil to draw a simple framework. You can start with a stick figure! Then add circles, ovals, and cylinders to get the basic form. Getting the simple shapes in place is the beginning to solving any great case.

Step 2: Time to add to Sherlock's look. Use the shapes you started with to fill in his clothes. Use guidelines to add circles for the eyes. And don't forget the hair.

Step 3: Now you can go in with a pen and start inking Sherlock. Fill in all the details and fix any mistakes. Let the ink dry to avoid smudges, then erase any pencil marks. Sherlock is ready for some color, so grab your markers and get started!

Glossary

bequest - request made in a will.

breastpin - a decorative pin.

bullion - bars of gold or silver.

commonplace - something commonly found

dissolve - to bring to an end.

eligible - having everything needed to participate in an activity or group if chosen.

forfeit - lose the right to something by making an error or committing a crime.

Freemason - a member of an organization that has secret rituals.

ingenious - having originality and cleverness.

pawnbroker - a person who lends money in exchange for personal property.

pound - an English coin equal to 12 shillings. Twelve shillings weigh one pound (.5 kg).

reasoned - to make a conclusion based on orderly rational thoughts.

solicitor - a British lawyer.

tradesman - a worker in the business of buying and selling things.

unique - being the only one of its kind.

vacancy - an empty spot.

Web Sites

To learn more about Sir Arthur Conan Doyle, visit ABDO Group online at **www.abdopublishing.com**. Web sites about Doyle are featured on our Book Links page. These links are routinely monitored and updated to provide the most current information available.

About the Author

Arthur Conan Doyle was born on May 22, 1859, in Edinburgh, Scotland. He was the second of Charles Altamont and Mary Foley Doyle's ten children. In 1868, Conan Doyle began his schooling in England. Eight years later, he returned to Scotland.

Upon his return, Doyle entered the University of Edinburgh's medical school, where he became a doctor in 1885. That year, he married Louisa Hawkins. Together they had two children.

While a medical student, Doyle was impressed when his professor observed the tiniest details of a patient's condition. Doyle later wrote stories where his most famous character, Sherlock Holmes, used this same technique to solve mysteries. Holmes first appeared in *A Study in Scarlet* in 1887 and was immediately popular.

Between 1887 and 1927, Doyle wrote 66 stories and 3 novels about Holmes. He also wrote other fiction and nonfiction novels throughout his life. In 1902, Doyle was knighted for his work in a field hospital in the South African War. Four years later, Louisa died. Doyle married Jean Leckie in 1907, and they had three children together.

Sir Arthur Conan Doyle died on July 7, 1930, in Sussex, England. Today, Doyle's famous character, Sherlock Holmes, is honored with societies around the world that pay tribute to the detective.

Additional Works

A Study in Scarlet (1887)

The Mystery of Cloomber (1889)

The Firm of Girdlestone (1890)

The White Company (1891)

The Adventures of Sherlock Holmes (1891-92)

The Memoirs of Sherlock Holmes (1892-93)

Round the Red Lamp (1894)

The Stark Munro Letters (1895)

The Great Boer War (1900)

The Hound of the Baskervilles (1901-02)

The Return of Sherlock Holmes (1903-04)

Through the Magic Door (1907)

The Crime of the Congo (1909)

The Coming of the Fairies (1922)

Memories and Adventures (1924)

The Case-Book of Sherlock Holmes (1921-1927)

About the Adapters

Author

Vincent Goodwin earned his B.A. in Drama and Communications from Trinity University in San Antonio. He is the writer of three plays as well as the co-writer of the comic book *Pirates vs. Ninjas II*. Goodwin is also an accomplished journalist, having won several awards for his work as a columnist and reporter.

Illustrator

Ben Dunn founded Antarctic Press, one of the largest comic companies in the United States. His works appear in Marvel and Image comics. He is best known for his series *Ninja High School* and *Warrior Nun Areala*.